NIGHTWALKER 4

NIGHTWALKER 4

A POST-APOCALYPTIC WESTERN ADVENTURE

FRANK RODERUS

CRAIG MARTELLE

CHAPTER ONE

James Wolfe stood and took a long, careful look around. Finding no enemies, he picked up his rucksack and weapons. Wolfe was desperately trying to get home.

A nuclear holocaust had caught Wolfe in Idaho, thousands of miles from his home and – far more importantly – his family in Bradenton, Florida. The bombs shattered the United States, creating hot zones, red zones flooded with harmful radiation and clear areas where no radiation remained. Those zones were governed by a new entity called the Federal Command.

Wolfe had run afoul of some brothers, smugglers who scavenged manufactured goods from the radioactive Hot Zones. The Alston brothers had accused him of murder, and now Wolfe was a fugitive any time he was in a Clear Area.

Unfortunately, he was easy to identify by way of his mane of snowy white hair, part of the legacy from his activity immediately after the war. At that time, to escape the fallout from the bombs that targeted Boise, Wolfe holed up inside an old mine shaft. Subsisting on the foods that were in the long-haul truck he had been driving, he stayed there for more than two years.

Somehow, from radiation or due to strange chemical components in the water that seeped out of the walls, he had become immensely strong and quick. His hair had turned white and his beard no longer grew. He could also sense radiation as a tingle in his fingertips. That came in handy to keep him safe in the Hot Zone. The biggest change, however, was in his eyesight.

When Wolfe finally emerged from the Idaho mineshaft, he could see in the dark with all the acuity of a stalking cat, but was painfully blinded by daylight. He had scavenged a pair of welding goggles that he wore in daylight to cut the light and avoid the pain of exposure.

James Wolfe was greatly changed by the time he spent in that mine. But none of that mattered to him. All he cared about now was to get home to Lurleen and their toddler Jo-Jo, Joseph Henry Wolfe IV, named for Wolfe's father and grandfather.

Home to his family if he could find them.

Home to his family if they still lived.

With a deep sigh he shouldered his rucksack and his weapons – a pair of M16 rifles, a powerful bow, a blowgun and a sack of precious ammunition for the rifles – along with camp gear, a sleeping bag and a few items of clothing. It was more than most had. A treasure to be cherished or something to be coveted by others.

"C'mon, dog," he said, patting his thigh to summon the big dog that had attached itself to him during his travels. "We got miles to cover." Several thousand miles, actually, but that did not matter if he could only get through to find Lurleen and Jo-Jo.

Undaunted, he and his hairy traveling companion set out again.

CHAPTER TWO

"There we go, dog. Just what we need," Wolfe said, looking at a long abandoned gas station a half mile or so ahead. Minutes later he broke the door open and went inside. He found the map rack and pulled out one that covered Wyoming, Utah and Colorado.

With a sigh, Wolfe sat at the desk and spread the map open, trying to work out his best way forward.

Unfortunately, the map was printed pre-war and did not show where the Hot Zone ended and the more dangerous – to him – Clear Area began.

Wolfe knew he needed to avoid the cesspool of radiation that had been Salt Lake City and equally to avoid the string of danger zones that would have been Cheyenne, Denver, Colorado Springs and possibly Pueblo as well.

The radiation was one factor he had to consider. Water was another. And finding food was a logical third.

Immediately south was something called badlands. That did not sound very enticing. Nor did the Clear Area that he knew lay somewhere ahead.

Wolfe grunted aloud.

"We'll go on through South Pass," he mused to the big, German Shepherd cross, which sat and cocked its head to one side. "Turn south and unless we run into FedCom troopers go south through Colorado. I'm thinking by the time we get down into New Mexico we should be beyond danger from them. I wouldn't think their BOLOs should extend that far. In the meantime, next town we come to, I'll take out some insurance against them recognizing me."

Wolfe smiled and scratched the dog behind the ears, a gesture it seemed to especially enjoy.

"Come along," he said, patting his thigh to summon the dog. He picked up his gear and set off into the night at a fast walk.

An hour past dawn he came to Rock Springs or what was left of it. Most of what he could see had been vandalized. The rest was simply abandoned. If anyone remained here, Wolfe did not see them. More telling, the dog gave no indication of the presence of humans.

Wolfe found another gas station, this time looking up an address in the local telephone directory and again plucking a map from the display. With that to guide him, he walked to what had been a Walmart store.

It was bright daylight outside, but Wolfe was able to pull the welding goggles down and see perfectly well inside the cavernous store.

As he fully expected, nearly everything of value in the store had long since been picked over and carried away. Incredibly, even the flat screen televisions had been taken by scavengers – dreamers – who must have believed that electricity and commercial television would return someday.

He made his way first to the toy department and was pleased to find a bin that still contained small rubber balls in a variety of colors.

Wolfe picked out all the ones that fit into his blowgun.

Then he headed for the display of hair dyes. Those seemed to have been completely neglected by the vandals who took most of the merchandise. He picked out a nondescript brown shade and took all four packages that they had, one to use immediately and the remaining three to use when his roots began to show.

Then it was back to the kitchen wares. There was little remaining on those shelves, mostly small appliances that required electricity to operate. That was just fine by Wolfe. A blender provided him with a rather nice pitcher, and a mixer set gave him a dandy bowl to work with.

"Okay, dog," he said when he had those in hand. "Let's go find us some water so I can go back to having dark hair, shall we?"

The dog wagged its tail in assent and pricked its ears forward, waiting for Wolfe's next command.

CHAPTER THREE

Three days later, dawn caught them in the open. They were following a highway that was quickly reverting to cracks with weeds pushing through to daylight.

"There," Wolfe said, pointing to a culvert that would at least get him out of the direct sunlight. Not that the dog cared what he said or where he pointed, but talking with the animal as if it were a companion seemed to help.

He walked away from what was left of the pavement and made his way down a slight embankment to the shadowy opening.

"It's dry," he announced with pleasure, "and I don't see any snakes or other critters. What do you think?"

The dog made its opinion plain enough. It trotted over to the culvert mouth and cautiously walked inside.

Wolfe stashed his gear ahead of him as he crawled into the concrete tube, putting his precious belongings on the other side of his body and the culvert opening. He pulled his goggles over his eyes and curled up along the dank floor, promptly falling asleep.

Sometime later – he had no idea how long he might have slept – Wolfe was awakened by the dog's growling.

And a human voice telling him, "Just stay right there, mister. No sudden moves, hear? We got you covered." The man giggled. "With your own gun. Now isn't that a hoot?"

Wolfe looked at the dog. "Let me know sooner than now? I swear you are a lousy watch dog."

CHAPTER FOUR

"Are you sure you want to do this?" Wolfe calmly asked. "Mister, we already done it," the man with the rifle answered. "Now just stay right there. No need for you to bother y'self. Just get hold of your dog…I'd hate to have to shoot him…or you. So call him off and go back to sleep. We'll take care o' everything else." The man giggled and waved the rifle back and forth.

"You aren't going to shoot me with an empty rifle," Wolfe said.

"Huh?"

"Look for yourself."

The fellow with the weapon dropped his eyes to the rifle as if he could see whether it was loaded or not. It was, of course, but he did not know that.

Wolfe launched himself, moving with an almost super-human speed. He snatched the rifle by the barrel, yanking it out of the hands of the marauder. Just as quickly he dropped the rifle and took hold of the fellow's head with both hands. A quick twist and an ugly sound of shattering bone and the man's neck broke.

There were two others standing behind that one. Wolfe let the first man's body drop while he went after the nearer of the remaining two. He was aware of a gray flash at his right side as the dog charged out of the culvert too.

Wolfe grabbed the second man and jerked him so hard he could feel the arm break. The man howled in pain and went to his knees. At that he was better off than his companion.

The dog tore that man's throat out, blood gushing from the ragged wound in a torrent.

"Don't, mister, please don't," Wolfe's victim screamed.

His companion dropped, both hands clutching his throat in a futile attempt to stop the flow of blood.

"Don't hurt me, mister. Please," the man whined as he held his broken arm with his free hand. "Please."

Wolfe thought the dog looked rather pleased with itself. It came back to Wolfe and sat at his side while the fellow he had defended them against quickly bled to death.

The remaining marauder begged for his life.

"Get out of here," Wolfe snarled. "If I see you again, I'll kill you, understand?"

"Y-y-yes, sir," he stammered, then turned and fled without a backward glance toward his dead friends. Some friend. Marauders. Scavengers. Thieves.

The scum of the earth.

Wolfe picked up the rifle the first man had dropped and retrieved the backpack they intended to steal.

"Now there's a good sleep ruined, "Wolfe said as he shouldered the backpack "Come on, dog. We might as well do some traveling since we're awake anyway."

CHAPTER FIVE

Wolfe had been through Baggs, Wyoming several times when driving his long-haul truck. It was a town he always admired. He knew nothing about it, really, but always thought of it as a clean and pleasant community, one he might have enjoyed living in.

Now it seemed like no one lived there. The town appeared to be completely deserted.

Out of a sudden impulse of nostalgia, Wolfe stopped at the same café where he always used to when passing through. He had no illusions about being able to order food there, but it would be daybreak soon enough and it would not hurt to stop a little early for a change.

"What do you think, dog? Are you ready to get off your paws for a little while?"

The big dog looked at him and wagged its tail.

"You agree, do you? All right then. We'll stop here and get some rest while I think about what used to be, back in the day."

Wolfe pushed the café door open and walked inside. The place was very much as he remembered but a little dusty now and without the scents of frying food and the low burr of conversations.

He took a deep breath and sighed, then set his weapons down and swung the pack off his back.

"Take your choice for a place to sleep," he suggested aloud. "As for me, I think I'll rearrange that booth there so I can have those seat cushions to sleep on."

He pulled the table out of the way and pushed the two seats together to form a bed of sorts. It was too short which meant his legs hung over the end. But it would do. And in great comfort for someone accustomed to sleeping on the ground.

He stuffed his rifles between him and the wall and used his backpack as a pillow. It was not soft, but it was better than nothing.

The dog curled up close to his feet. Wolfe pulled his welder's goggles over his eyes, lay down and was quickly asleep.

CHAPTER SIX

The dog's growls woke him. Wolfe sat up. It was daylight but mercifully he had the dark goggles in place to protect his eyes.

The hackles at the back of the dog's neck were standing tall, and the big animal was poised protectively close to Wolfe, crouched ready to spring.

It took only a moment for him to see what the problem was. Beside the café door were two men. They each held a long gun. One carried a bolt-action hunting rifle and the other, a shotgun. Both wore rumpled camouflage clothing and were heavily bearded.

"Call off your dog, mister. We wouldn't want t' hurt him," the shorter of the two said.

Wolfe laid a hand on the dog's head, and it relaxed. A little. It dropped to a seat but maintained a wary vigilance at his side.

"Who are you and what do you want?" Wolfe asked.

"Seems to me we're the ones ought t' be asking questions, mister," the same man said. "Are you one o' the Leader's people?"

"I don't know any Leader," Wolfe said. "I'm not from around here. Just passing through, actually."

"Can you prove that?" the taller man demanded.

Wolfe scowled. "Now how on earth am I supposed to prove something like that?" he snapped. He was becoming irritated. These men were making demands and while they were not overtly threatening the mere fact that they held the guns served as threat enough.

He gauged the distance between himself, sitting on the edge of the booth cushions, and the men who were standing at the doorway. He wondered if he could reach and dispatch them before they could shoot or would he have to use his own rifle and try to get off a shot first.

It was a toss-up, Wolfe concluded. It depended on how quickly the two could react and bring the guns into play.

Wolfe scowled again and shifted closer to the edge of the seat, readying himself to make the jump.

The dog beside him obviously sensing what Wolfe was doing, tensed ready to spring when Wolfe did.

If they were only a few feet closer….

CHAPTER SEVEN

The two were about a half second from dying – and perhaps Wolfe with them – when the shorter man shrugged and slung the hunting rifle over his shoulder.

The man turned to his companion and said, "It's all right, Glenn."

"But what if…"

"We can't be suspicious of everybody," the short man said. He was obviously the leader of the two. Glenn balanced his shotgun over his shoulder, although he looked none too happy about it.

The shorter man turned back to Wolfe and said, "The Leader is…what would I call him? A local dictator? Or anyway someone who thinks he should be in charge of everything and everybody. You really don't know who he is?"

Wolfe shook his head. "I'm just passing through on my way home, me and this dog."

"And where would home be?" Glenn asked, obviously still suspicious of the stranger.

"Florida," Wolfe said. "Down on the Gulf coast. I, uh, don't suppose you've heard anything about the damage down that way?"

The short man shook his head. "Sorry."

"Are we inside the Federal Command's Clear Areas here?" Wolfe asked.

"We are." A moment later he added, "You look like that worries you."

Wolfe shrugged. "Just curious."

"If you say so." He yawned and stretched and said, "We don't have much we can offer you, mister. A little soup made out of seeds is about it. But you're welcome to share. Are you hungry?"

Wolfe grinned. "You bet."

"Then come along with us. We'll all of us put on the feedbag."

"There are more of you?"

"A little more than a dozen of us who've chosen to go our own way rather than knuckle under to the Leader."

Wolfe picked up his backpack and pair of rifles and followed the two local men out of the café and down a silent street, past abandoned pickup trucks and empty store fronts to what had been a sprawling school building.

"We're all living in here," the leader – whose name Wolfe still had not heard – said. "Safety in numbers, you see."

"What are you worried this Leader fellow might do anyway?" Wolfe asked.

"That's the thing. We don't know. But he scares us, that's for sure."

"We all of us grew up pretty much together," Glenn said. "We knew Daniel before he decided he was the Leader. He was always a bully and a know-it-all. The war just gave him an excuse to get even worse."

"Come in now and meet our tribe," the short man said, pushing the glass door open and motioning Wolfe inside.

CHAPTER EIGHT

There were seventeen of them, counting Glenn and his companion, seven men and ten women. Their ages ranged, Wolfe guessed, from mid-teens to elderly, the women being younger and the men more toward the elderly side.

The short man, the leader of this group but not The Leader, introduced them by name, but Wolfe did not catch most of them. The only name he was sure of was a woman who was probably in her early thirties. Melinda was slender to the point of being gaunt – as most of these people were – with dark hair and huge, flashing eyes. Had it not been for his beloved Lurleen back home in Florida he would have been interested in Melinda. And judging by the way she looked at him he was fairly sure that she was interested in him.

"I invited Mr. Wolfe here to have dinner with us."

Despite the obvious poverty of these people no one objected to a stranger partaking of some of their precious food.

"Gather 'round, folks," the leader said – Wolfe was beginning to think he was the one who should be calling himself the Leader – "and let's have breakfast."

The group of survivors arranged themselves in a circle. Melinda managed to place herself next to Wolfe. Without having to be told, everyone took the hands of whoever stood next to them. Melinda's hand was small and light in Wolfe's. The touch of her made him miss Lurleen all the more.

Again without needing a command they bowed their heads, and the leader launched into a softly spoken prayer of thanks for the fact that they had a hot meal to enjoy.

The soup was warm in his belly but not exactly filling. It was no wonder, Wolfe thought, that all of these people were so thin. The substance of the soup, what little there was of it, appeared to be grass seeds along with crunchy bits that he suspected were ants or some other variety of bug. He decided he did not really want to know what those were.

"I'm sorry we had no meat to offer," the leader said when they were done. The men set about washing their bowls and utensils while the women took plastic grocery sacks and left.

"They will spend the rest of the day gathering seeds or whatever looks edible," the short man explained, "then come back here to cook supper."

"And what do you men do during the day?" Wolfe asked.

"We have slingshots. You know. The kind King David used to slay Goliath."

"You don't have firearms or bows to hunt with?" Wolfe asked.

"No, Daniel and his people grabbed up all of those before we thought to arm ourselves."

Wolfe nodded then said, "Would you mind if I lie down for a little sleep while you are out? I walk at night and sleep during the day, and today I was, um, interrupted."

"You go right ahead, friend. There are lots of rooms in the school where you can find some privacy. Meanwhile we'll go out and see what we can find to add to the larder."

CHAPTER NINE

Wolfe slept for two hours or so, then got up and found his way out of the sprawling building. He took only his blowgun and a handful of rubber ball darts.

Several hours later when the local folk returned they found Wolfe sitting amid a pile of feathers and with a baker's dozen of small birds already cleaned.

"Something to add to the pot," he said.

"But how did you get them? We've given up trying to take them with our slingshots. They just aren't accurate enough," the leader said.

Wolfe motioned to his blowgun lying nearby.

"With that tube thing?"

He nodded. "It's just a piece of conduit. You can find it everywhere. But it serves just fine as a blowgun, and once you get used to it, it's pretty accurate, as you can see from these. Actually the dog helps. He makes a commotion, and the birds sitting up on the wires pay attention to him and not to me. Then I get underneath them and pick them off the wires fairly easily. I don't usually take so many of them, but then usually I'm feeding just the dog and myself."

"We'll be glad to have these, believe me. And will you please show us how you do this? I think in the future we'll be eating a lot better thanks to you." The short man turned to the women and said, "Ellie, come get these birds and add them to the soup."

"Oh, yes, Jason. They will make a wonderful broth, and there may even be a little meat for each of us."

Ha! Wolfe thought. Jason. The man's name was Jason.

Ellie and two other women, Melinda included, came over and collected the birds from Wolfe and carried them away to the kitchen.

The group ate well that evening.

CHAPTER TEN

"Aluminum conduit works best," Wolfe explained to the menfolk. "You can use PVC, but it's heavy. I don't like it personally, but use whatever you can find."

He motioned to the walls around them. "Wherever there are electric wires running through a wall you can likely find conduit. A few swipes with a hacksaw and you have your blowgun all ready to go."

"What about the darts?" a man named Elliott asked. "Are those rubber balls you're using?"

Wolfe nodded. "Got these from a Walmart, but you can probably find something similar in a five and dime or a CVS store, almost anywhere. Another possibility would be the little balls attached to paddles. Just take them off and put a nail through them to make the dart. Or a long sliver of wood. That works too. You don't need much to bring down a bird. Rabbits are a little harder. I use my bow for those." He smiled and shrugged. "Squirrels are almost impossible. They're tremendously strong and cling to life like no other creature. Leave them alone would be my suggestion."

"What about antelope, deer and the like?" someone else asked.

"Not with a blowgun, and you probably won't be able to get close enough to use a bow. If you don't have a firearm, I'd say to leave those alone."

The man who had asked the question looked disappointed.

"I want each of you to try using this blowgun. We won't put nails or splinters into the balls. Just fire the balls by themselves to get used to it." Wolfe passed around his blowgun and a handful of small rubber balls so each man in the tribe could try his hand.

The evening was spent in laughter and camaraderie as the aluminum tube went from hand to hand...and the men discovered just how badly they missed their targets firing the rubber balls.

"I think a good deal of practice will be in order once we're all armed," Jason observed as he handed the blowgun on to the next man in the circle.

CHAPTER ELEVEN

"Ladies, that was a fine supper. Thank you." Wolfe rose from the cafeteria table and carried his tray to the kitchen. He was not exaggerating. The songbird soup had been hot and filling and reasonably tasty.

"Just set your tray there," one of the women told him. "We'll take care of it."

"We don't have much in the way of a nightlife," Jason apologized. "We ran out of lamp oil months ago so anything we do has to be done in the dark."

"You know what?" Wolfe said. "I'd bet there must be a thousand gallons of diesel fuel in the underground tanks at the truck stop over on the edge of town. Remind me tomorrow morning. I'll pull the cover on it and see how much is there. Likely enough to fuel your lamps and lanterns for years."

"Good Lord, yes. Why didn't any of us think of that?" Jason responded. "When the electricity failed and the pumps no longer worked we kind of thought that was that. But if you can get the fuel out of the ground…"

"I'm sure I can," Wolfe said. He smiled. "In the morning.

So get your lamps ready. For now though, I for one am off to bed. I bid you all a fond good night."

He motioned for the dog to join him, picked up his blowgun and headed for the comfortable room that now seemed to be his, complete with a mattress that someone had brought in for his use.

CHAPTER TWELVE

Lurleen. Lord, how he missed her.

Wolfe woke sometime during the night after going to bed on the schedule of the local tribe. It was a courtesy to his hosts even though he normally traveled at night. He woke thinking – dreaming – of his wife, who, if she lived, was still thousands of miles away.

He could as good as feel Lurleen lying warm and gentle at his side, her body pressing softly against his. Wolfe's body responded as it had a thousand times during their marriage.

He turned to her. Slid his hand across her waist, as she lay with her back and buttocks tight against him. Took hold of the softness of her. Felt the stirrings of an intense desire.

She opened herself to him, as she had so many times before, and he entered her sweet and willing body.

When he returned to sleep it was deep and restful, and his dreams were of Lurleen and Jo-Jo and the joys of home and family.

It was far and away the best sleep he had had in months.

CHAPTER THIRTEEN

Good Lord!

Wolfe sat bolt upright, startled that the first thing he saw when he woke in the morning was a head of dark hair.

Lurleen was blonde.

Melinda was sleeping at his side. And she was, as far as he could see, completely naked.

She was pressed tight against him, and when he moved she reached for him and tried to draw him closer.

"Good morning, lover," she cooed. "Come here, sweetheart. Let's do it again."

Wolfe felt sick to his stomach. He had traveled all over the country, was away from home for weeks and sometimes months at a time, but he had never been with another woman since the day he gave Lurleen his pledge of love and fidelity.

He had met a great many women in that time, some of them attractive, some even enticing. But he had never strayed.

Now...

He bolted from the mattress, leaving Melinda with a questioning look marring her pretty features.

Wolfe could have made excuses for himself. He had been groggy with sleep. He had thought Melinda was his own beloved Lurleen. He had…he had cheated on his wife was what he had done.

Excuses aside, for the rest of his days, James Wolfe would not be able to think of himself as a faithful husband.

He threw on his clothes, pulled the welding goggles over his eyes, picked up his blowgun and a fistful of darts and made his way out of the sprawling school building, moving practically at a run in his haste to escape what he had done. There was no escape, however, from himself. The man in the mirror would always know.

CHAPTER FOURTEEN

By the end of the day Wolfe had almost forty small birds cleaned and ready for the pot. He used his knife to remove the plump little breasts and set those aside. When he returned to the communal kitchen – Melinda was not there at the moment, thank goodness – he handed the breasts to the lady who seemed to be in charge and said, "Grill these. There's enough for everyone to have two and get some real meat for a change." He smiled. "Not much meat but at least some. And these," he pointed to the pile of carcasses, "can go in the pot. They'll make a fine broth from the scraps and bones."

"Wonderful. We have seeds and herbs that will go with the broth," the woman said. "By the way, Mr. Wolfe, Melinda was looking for you this afternoon. Do you want me to find her for you?"

Wolfe shook his head. "Thanks, but no. Not right now."

He had had all day to think about it and still did not know what he should do or say to Melinda the next time he saw her.

He turned and started out of the kitchen only to come face to face with the woman.

"I've been looking for you, lover." She came onto tiptoes to give him a kiss, a kiss that went far beyond mere friendliness.

"Look, uh, I don't know how to say this exactly, but last night…."

"Last night was wonderful," Melinda injected.

Wolfe took Melinda by the shoulders and gently pushed her away. "Last night was a mistake. I'm a married man, you know. I have a wife and a son back home that I'm trying to get to. I've never…in my whole life I've never, um…what I'm trying to say…."

"You don't have to say it," Melinda snapped, sudden anger distorting her features and darkening her complexion.

She spun on her heels and stalked away.

It was not a pleasant experience, Wolfe thought, but at least it was done.

He picked up his things and went back to the room he had been given in the sprawling school building.

CHAPTER FIFTEEN

The entire tribe was gathered together in the dining hall enjoying the scraps of meat Wolfe had provided and the hearty soup that went with it when suddenly the room became unnaturally silent.

All eyes were turned toward the doorway. Wolfe turned to see what the others were looking at so intently.

Uniforms! Men in the dark uniforms of the Federal Command police.

His heart skipped a beat, and he felt like there was some obstruction in his throat that kept him from breathing. His weapons were back in his room. Still, if he had to fight then fight he would, with his bare hands if it came to that.

The police – there were three of them so perhaps Wolfe could take them with sheer speed and power if it came to a fight – stalked into the room without invitation.

One of the men walked over to the serving line and lifted the lid on the big pot that held their soup. The man lifted the ladle and tasted the soup, then poured some of the broth into a bowl and drank from it.

With a grunt of approval he set the bowl down and walked through the room, staring at each individual in turn.

When he came to Wolfe he barely paused. Wolfe thanked God above that he had colored his hair. If a 'be on the look-out' warning had gone around the region's police barracks it would have been for a man with snowy white hair. Wolfe's hair was now a nondescript brown thanks to Miss Clairol.

He was worried that the presence of the dog might give him away, but the dog was back in his room as well. Good thing, he thought, else the faithful animal was sure to react to the police. Still, if the FedCom goons went room to room in the building he would either have to fight them or run away…and he would not do that without the dog and his gear. In that order.

Two of the police stood at the entrance while the leader strutted through the room peering at everyone.

Finally they left.

Jason looked at Wolfe with a little grin and laid a finger across his lips, inclining his head toward the doorway.

Wolfe got the message. The police were not really gone yet. They were just outside, listening.

Everyone went back to eating but in total silence now. The easy flow of conversation that had filled the room earlier was gone now.

After five minutes or so, one of the men – Wolfe thought the man's name was Charles, but he was not sure about that – went to the entry and peered out, then left the room and was gone for several minutes.

When Charles came back he nodded and said, "They're gone now. Pulled out for Daniel's compound."

Wolfe turned to Jason and said, "Do they do this very often?"

Jason shrugged. "They come through about once a month to check on us. I was afraid they might spot you as a stranger, but I guess they didn't." He chuckled. "I don't think they are really very much interested in us. What they really want is to get to Daniel's bunch."

"Why would they do that?" Wolfe asked.

"Women. The girls who went with Daniel are on the wild side. The FedComs always make it a point to reach Daniel in the evening. They spend the night there and move on in the morning."

"Really," Wolfe said, thinking. After a minute or so he said, "Where exactly is Daniel's compound anyway?"

"It's a couple miles east of here. The place used to be a dude ranch. A real ranch before that. They know we're no threat to them and we all used to be neighbors so they leave us alone."

"How many are there?"

Jason shrugged. "I don't know for sure. Forty or so would be my guess."

Wolfe smiled. "And three FedCom police tonight to go with those forty."

"For what that's worth, yes."

"Thanks." Wolfe finished his meal quickly, excused himself from the usual after-dinner conversation and returned to his room.

CHAPTER SIXTEEN

Wolfe closed the dog inside his room. It was not that he worried the animal would give him away. His concern was that the dog might feel compelled to take a bite out of someone. Better to leave well enough alone, he thought.

Once it was full dark out, Wolfe slipped his goggles down around his neck, freeing his vision to probe the night and make possible the little journey he had in mind for the evening.

With a quiet smile tugging at his lips, Wolfe left the former school building and, carrying no weapons except his knife, started east.

By the time he had gone two miles he could see a glow a half mile or so ahead. He walked toward it, but cautiously now. When he was a few hundred yards distant he could hear the sounds of revelry. Someone was having a party, and he could guess who that might be.

Daniel's compound was a collection of cottages, sheds and a large barn. The barn was where the party was taking place.

There was – Wolfe was surprised – electric light streaming out of the wide-open barn door.

Intrigued, he looked for the source and was pleased when he found it. A small windmill, probably originally intended to be a garden decoration, was turning a generator taken from an automobile. The lights then were likely twelve-volt bulbs scavenged from a car or truck.

And it worked nicely. Wolfe intended to take that suggestion back to the tribe at the school. They could surely make their own arrangement.

That, however, was not what he had come for.

He found the vehicle the FedCom police had arrived in. It was a small van, electric, which could transport prisoners in a cage in the back.

The police had left their rifles inside the cage. The cage was secured with a padlock and hasp at the rear.

Smiling, Wolfe took hold of the padlock and pulled, applying pressure until something inside broke.

He removed the padlock and set it aside on the rear bumper of the little van then helped himself to an M16 and a vinyl container that held, or so the lid said, fifteen hundred rounds of .223 caliber cartridges.

He took the rifle and ammunition then carefully replaced the padlock in the hasp. Likely when the lock was discovered broken they would think it had been defective to begin with. Until the rifle was found to be missing, that is. Then all Hell would break loose in Daniel's compound.

Wolfe set the carton of cartridges aside and took the M16 into one after another of the cottages until he found a civilian AR15 imitator of the M16, took it and left the stolen M16 in its place.

When the switch was discovered it would cause confusion at the very least and criminal charges at the worst. But whatever happened, it would be Daniel and his tribe who were blamed.

Wolfe tucked the AR15 under his arm, returned to the FedCom van and collected the carton of cartridges.

Behind him the party continued to rock in the big barn. There was even loud music courtesy of the automotive electric system and a CD or MP3 player, also automotive.

Yes, sir, he thought, *Jason's tribe was really going to like all this.*

Carrying his nocturnal 'purchases' and whistling a merry tune under his breath, Wolfe walked back to the former school building.

CHAPTER SEVENTEEN

"My God, Wolfe. Two rifles! And all these cartridges," Jason enthused. "I can't believe you would just give them to us."

"Minus a couple hundred rounds of ammunition that I'm keeping, but you get the rest," Wolfe said. "I want to keep those. But I do have spare M16s. I'm going to leave those with you too. I thought it over, and you folks can use these rifles. If you use them judiciously, the ammo should last you quite a while.

"I wouldn't recommend that you use up cartridges on small stuff like squirrels and rabbits, but you can bring down antelope…excuse me, pronghorns I think they are properly called…and the deer you can find in the brakes. Lots of meat on those." He smiled. "I think your people will be eating better from now on. I hope so anyway."

"We owe you," Jason said.

"Not at all."

"Actually, Wolfe, we talked this over while you were gone. We would like you to join our tribe. You would be a most welcome addition."

"That's nice of you and your people, Jason, and I thank you from the bottom of my heart. But I have to at least try to make it back to Florida. I have no idea if my wife and son are still alive and, if they are, where they are. But I have to look for them. I have to find them if they are alive somewhere and looking for me to come to them."

"You'll be leaving us then?"

Wolfe nodded. "As soon as I can collect my things."

"If you reconsider…"

"Thank you. Really. Thank you very much, all of you."

"Will you think it over at least?"

"There's nothing to think over, Jason. I have to get home. Or die trying. I hope you understand that."

Wolfe spent a few minutes explaining what he had seen of the electric lights and music and how to get them. He thought more about it and although he wanted to leave right away, there was one last bit of unfinished business.

"Grab that bucket and follow me," Wolfe said and walked away. The two went to the station where Wolfe thought he could get some of the diesel fuel from the tank. Although it would not be any good for a vehicle because it would go bad, it would burn just fine in a lamp. They pried off the cap for the underground tank. Wolfe stuck his face over it and breathed deeply. He closed his eyes and embraced the smell of diesel fuel. It brought good memories. When he opened his eyes, he found Jason staring at him.

"I drove long haul. Smelled a lot of diesel in my day. Grab that garden hose over there and let's see if we can get this thing done."

A one hundred foot hose would be tough to make work, but Wolfe wanted to give it a try. The good people trying to make a go at a new life deserved better than to sit in the dark. Wolfe dropped one end of the hose into the tank and then pulled it back up.

"Eight foot drop," he guessed. By the front of the station between it and the road, there was a ditch. "That should do it. We need this end to be lower than the one in the tank. Hold this in place."

Jason held the hose steady, letting it settle a few inches into the diesel. Wolfe stretched the hose until he was at the bottom of the ditch then he started swinging the end around in a circle, faster and faster. After about twenty seconds he heard the gurgle and then the fuel started spraying out. He slapped the end into the ground so it stayed lower than the tank, hurrying to get the bucket under it. When it filled, he lifted the hose to funnel the remaining fuel back into the tank.

He explained to Jason how to do it, and they traded places. Once Jason showed he knew how, they shook hands and returned to the school. Wolfe headed for the room where the dog and his gear were waiting.

Wolfe wanted to resume their march south.

CHAPTER EIGHTEEN

"Jim. Wait." Melinda was standing in the hallway when Wolfe and the dog emerged from his room.

"Jim, please."

"What is it, Mel?" He softened his expression a little and then smiled. "Is it all right if I call you that?"

Melinda laughed. "Really, Jim. We slept together last night. It isn't like we need to be formal with each other now. Of course it is okay. You can call me pretty much anything you like. Just listen to me for a minute."

"All right." He set his backpack on the floor and leaned his rifle against it. The dog settled on its haunches beside the pack, guarding its master's gear, not that anything needed guarding here, but the dog was ready if need be.

"I understand about your wife, Jim. You're a good and faithful husband, and I admire that. I really do. There aren't many like you anymore. But surely you know that your family was killed in the war.

"Florida is loaded with military places. Was loaded, I mean. Surely the whole state was blasted to smithereens by all those atom bombs.

"But, Jim, if you give me a chance I can be a good wife to you too. I'd be faithful. I would do everything for you. Everything. Anything. Just name it and I will do it.

"Stay here, Jim. Stay with us, and let me be your wife. We can get Jason to…I don't know. Give you a declaration as a single man, then marry us if that makes you feel better, or I would live with you as if a wife in every way. But stay here, I'm begging you. Stay with me."

Melinda took him by the arm and peered up into his face, her expression intense. The woman clearly meant what she was saying.

Wolfe leaned down and gently kissed her on the forehead, then just as gently removed her hand from his arm.

"You may be right, Mel. You probably are. But until I know different, I am still married to my Lurleen, and nothing can really change that."

Tears began to flow from Melinda's wide-open eyes. Her crying seemed somehow even more intense for the fact that she wept in complete silence, without sobbing or otherwise displaying the misery that overtook her.

"I'm sorry," Wolfe said. He picked up his pack and slung it onto his back.

A quick motion of his hand and the dog was at his side, both of them eager to be on their way and make the most of what was left of the night.

"Good-bye, Mel."

Melinda did not answer as Wolfe turned away and left the relative comforts of Jason's tribe.

He had done what he could to help them in the few days he had spent with them. It was up to them to use what he had given them to better their lives, whether hunting big game with the rifles, small game with the blowguns, or working under diesel-fueled lamps.

Within minutes they – and Baggs – were out of sight behind him.

CHAPTER NINETEEN

"Those are good people back there, dog," Wolfe said as he marched resolutely on. "I wish them well."

The dog responded to his voice with a wag of its tail.

Near dawn, with the eastern sky beginning to pale, Wolfe exchanged the rifle in his hands for his bow and a brace of arrows. He strapped the rifle to the side of his backpack where the bow had been.

"Now to find us some breakfast." He smiled. "Or supper, depending on how you want to look at it."

The dog wagged some more.

They walked on, but slower now, until Wolfe spotted three rabbits grazing in a clearing. He motioned for the dog to sit, which it obediently did.

He eased a little closer to the rabbits then sent a carefully aimed arrow flying. The nearest rabbit was skewered; the other two disappeared in a heartbeat.

"It looks like we have our meal," Wolfe said aloud. He made a throwing motion and the dog loped forward. It found the dead rabbit and brought it back to Wolfe, arrow and all.

"Half for you and half for me," Wolfe said as he set his pack down and withdrew the knife from his belt.

CHAPTER TWENTY

"Aaaaaaa!"

Wolfe cried out, startled, and grunted when his head hit the ground. Hard. He heard a dull thud that drove deep in his skull.

The next thing he knew it was daylight, and his goggles were still down around his neck. He must have been out for more than an hour.

The direct, unfiltered sunlight felt like his eyeballs were being stabbed. He quickly reached for the goggles at his neck and pulled them up over his eyes.

That was better but he was pretty sure he had broken something. His left leg hurt like crazy, and there was a throbbing in his head along with a sound like buzzing bees.

The dog was lying close at his side. It whimpered a little when Wolfe stirred.

"It's all right, boy," Wolfe said. "I hope." He added those last words in a hoarse whisper.

"Stupid smart aleck," he chided himself.

The road he was following south through Colorado zigzagged down a steep hillside. Thinking to save himself some steps and not really being required to stay on the road, Wolfe had chosen to walk straight downhill.

That was a mistake.

The hill was steeper than he realized and the footing treacherous.

He slipped on the loose rock and fell hard. Worse, trying to avoid falling back on his rucksack and trying to protect the rifle in his hand, he twisted to the side and went down hard on his left side then banged his head against some rocks. All in all, not his best of days.

"Idiot," he grumbled aloud and stood up.

And promptly fell down again when his left leg buckled and a bolt of sheer agony shot through it.

Broken? Sprained? Deep bruise? He had no idea what the damage was, but he was not going to be walking on that leg for a while.

"Come here, boy," Wolfe said, gritting his teeth against the pain and draping an arm over the nervous dog's back. "Go get Timmy, boy. Fetch help."

The dog licked his face, not understanding the command from long before its lifetime, and Wolfe scratched it behind the ears.

"I think," Wolfe said, "we're going to be here for a while."

CHAPTER TWENTY-ONE

With the dog for some physical support – and a good bit of comfort as well – Wolfe struggled into a sitting position.

He removed his backpack with the bow strapped on one side and his blowgun on the other. He pulled the bulky pack around into his lap, laying it across his knees and placing his rifle on top of it. Then he began carefully, slowly scooting down the hill on his backside.

He thought wistfully about Jason's tribe of survivors back in Baggs, but he was several days gone from the comforts of human companionship and long out of their reach.

Melinda would have been happy to take care of him while he healed, he thought with a small smile. More than happy. He sighed and concentrated on the problems at hand.

It took Wolfe the better part of two hours to reach the bottom of the hill.

A thin stream, flanked by tall grass and softly marshy banks, ran there.

When he finally reached the bottom Wolfe again tried

standing. With no better result. He simply could put no weight on his left leg.

He did not think the bone was broken. At least he could feel no break. He certainly could feel extreme pain there, though.

"It's no go, dog. Not for a while anyhow."

The dog sat close beside him, and Wolfe put an arm around its shoulders for a moment, then lay back and closed his eyes. He needed sleep anyway. And time to heal. He just hoped the leg would feel better when he woke.

CHAPTER TWENTY-TWO

"Oh, Lord!" Wolfe cried out as a bolt of sheer agony shot through his leg. This time he felt broken bone ends shift, and his leg took on a curve that Nature had not intended.

Wolfe passed out cold. When he woke it was night, and he could pull the goggles down.

He examined the leg as best he could. What he really needed was a doctor and a hospital. Did such things as public hospitals still exist? He had no idea. What he did know was that there was no such thing here where he lay nor any other human he could turn to for help. Whatever he did he would have to do it on his own.

"Are you hungry, dog? Me too. Don't know what we can do about it right now though, so tighten your belt and be patient. We'll work this out. Somehow."

That was the optimistic view of things, he realized. Maybe he would work it out. Or maybe he would lie here until he starved to death and the dog could go off on its own.

"How come you didn't get Timmy for me, eh?" he said,

rubbing the dog's head and ears fondly. "Or at least bring Lassie. She could do the job. Be a fine date for you too."

Wolfe sat up and looked around. On the far side of the stream there was a thick stand of aspen on a hillside. That had the potential to provide him with firewood and perhaps with shelter as well.

If he could get there.

CHAPTER TWENTY-THREE

L ord, that creek water was cold.

In order to reach the aspen, Wolfe had no choice but to cross the stream. And, unable to stand or to walk, he had no choice either except to crawl.

Damn water was icy cold. And, well, wet.

Dragging his backpack with his weapons strapped to it, he inched his way into the water and through it to the far side.

Once on the far bank he continued to crawl, careful to avoid pushing with the broken leg, up the slope and into the aspen grove.

By the time he reached the aspen he was soaked through and was shivering violently.

He stifled a whimper of pain and lay quiet, the dog still at his side.

"If you want to go find something to eat it would be all right," he said. Not that the dog would understand, but he felt better for saying it.

"As for me, I just want to rest here a while before we do anything else. Is that all right with you, dog?"

Wolfe put his head down on his folded arms and tried to sleep. He was not looking forward to what he had to do next.

CHAPTER TWENTY-FOUR

Wolfe wriggled deeper into the aspen grove until he found a pair of young trees growing side by side, their roots close together and the trunks almost forming a V-shape where they came out of the ground. That was not what he wanted but it was certainly what he needed.

Wolfe steeled himself and picked up his left leg, shoving forward and then pressing down until his hiking boot was lodged firmly between the trees.

He found a scrap of dead wood on the ground at his side and clamped that between his teeth lest he bite down so hard as to break a tooth.

Then came the hard part. Wolfe closed his eyes, planted his right foot against the trees.

And pushed.

A lightning bolt of agony unlike anything he had ever known drove through him.

He pushed as hard as he could manage despite the pain. Kept pushing until he felt the bone ends pull and shift and come together.

Only when he had accomplished that did James Wolfe allow himself the relief of unconsciousness.

CHAPTER TWENTY-FIVE

Wolfe waited until the pain in his leg had diminished to mere throbbing with the flow of blood pumping through his arteries, then took his backpack off and brought it around to his lap, his foot still jammed tight between the boles of the two aspens.

He thought carefully about what he could afford to lose, then removed his spare shirt from the pack. He took out his knife and cut the sleeve away from the shirt then carefully cut that into strips. He did the same with the other sleeve.

Nearby blowdown provided enough wood for splints, and the strips of flannel allowed him to tie the splints in place, two pieces of brittle aspen wood on each side of the broken leg.

Wolfe did not feel a bit better after the splint was tied in place but he knew it was necessary if he wanted the leg to heal. And he still had a very long way to go on that leg.

"Now," he said. "What are we going to do about supper?"

The dog wagged its tail, apparently agreeable to whatever Wolfe decided in that regard.

"Food," he said, again aloud. "We need food, don't we? So how does fish sound to you?"

He rummaged in his backpack for a coil of fishing line and plastic pack of small hooks.

With the splint on his leg he was able to crawl more easily. He made his way slowly, very slowly, downhill, out of the aspens and into some tall grass. There he caught three small grasshoppers.

With those he figured he was in business as a fisherman.

Halfway down to the stream, which he most seriously hoped contained some pan fish, he saw a trio of cow elk coming down to water.

Wolfe put his hand on the dog's neck to keep it from chasing the animals and mumbled, "This is a fine time to've left the rifle behind, isn't it? Well, that's the last time I'll make that mistake."

When the elk had had their drink and moved on, Wolfe and the dog continued their slow, painful trek down to the creek.

It would be daylight soon. And Wolfe was hungry.

CHAPTER TWENTY-SIX

By several hours past dawn he had three small fish. Coming from Florida, he knew a bit about fishing, but those were saltwater species. He had no idea what these three might be. But whatever they were, he intended to eat them.

Wolfe sat up and coiled his fishing line then slipped it into his shirt pocket. "One for you," he said to the dog, "one for me and we split the last one. How does that sound to you?"

He took out his knife and cleaned the three fish then crawled laboriously back up the slope to where he had left his things. He gathered some twigs and small sticks together and used a magnifying glass to start a fire. He still had several butane cigarette lighters in his pack but wanted to save those since it was daylight and there was sunshine enough to use the magnifying glass.

Wolfe dug into his backpack again for the one cooking utensil he carried, a small skillet. He had no grease to properly fry the fish in but searing them on hot metal would have to do.

A half hour later he was still hungry but much more comfortable than he had been with a completely empty belly. Wolfe gave the dog a pat, then stretched out in the grass and went to sleep, goggles firmly in place over his eyes.

CHAPTER TWENTY-SEVEN

"Damn," Wolfe muttered when he woke up. His little campsite, such as was, was covered with a thin dusting of snow. And if he was to judge by the dark clouds rolling in from the north there was more to come.

Crawling, straining, and reaching, he managed to come up with some slender saplings that he laboriously chopped down with his knife and, farther uphill, he reached a stand of older growth that sported some well-needled pine branches.

He chose the two shortest saplings and planted them into the ground, using the knife to dig out holes to receive them, then laid the longer saplings across these at about waist height and leaned the rest of the saplings onto this horizontal support.

The pine boughs were placed onto the saplings, effectively forming a lean-to.

Wolfe moved his few things into the shelter and built a fire just outside the mouth of the lean-to. The sun had long since set so he had to use one of his precious butane lighters to start the fire, but under the circumstances he considered heat more important than frugality.

The hillside and dead aspen provided fuel for the fire, and once he was inside the lean-to with a fire blazing just outside the mouth he was not only warm, he was uncomfortably hot.

That brought a smile of appreciation to his weather tanned face. He had read about such structures but had never before actually built one.

"Come on in here, dog. It's close quarters but there should be room enough for both of us." He dropped another stick onto the fire and said, "Sorry, but we're going to bed hungry tonight. Maybe tomorrow, eh?"

The dog wagged its tail and lay down, curling into a hairy ball when it did so.

"I wish I could do that too," Wolfe said with a grin. "All right now. Let's us both get some sleep and hope that tomorrow will be better."

CHAPTER TWENTY-EIGHT

The second day he lay in wait where the elk came down to drink.

One well-placed shot and he had a cow on the ground. He could not run to finish her off, but he could crawl. And got there while she was still thrashing around and whistling.

"Cold as it is, we'll as good as have the meat refrigerated, dog."

With considerable difficulty Wolfe skinned the animal – which probably provided several hundred pounds of meat – and cut the carcass into manageable pieces.

He removed the bladders and used the urine from them to dress the flesh side of the skin. Using the uric acid was not an ideal form of tanning, but it would have to do.

He left the pelt to cure overnight while he made trips up to the lean-to carrying meat. There was enough of it to fill his backpack several times. He saved the best – the liver – for last. That night he feasted on fire-grilled liver until he could eat no more.

The dog ate its fill also. They were a contented pair when they dropped off to sleep at daybreak the next morning.

Wolfe spent several days cutting the meat into thin strips for drying and hanging the meat across the fans – fronds? he was not sure what they were called – of some low growing juniper.

It was just as well that he was a nocturnal animal himself because he stayed awake to protect their supply of meat and twice had to warn off an inquisitive and possibly hungry bear that came calling.

Their food supply, though, was in hand, and Wolfe breathed a little easier.

By their third week huddling under the lean-to it was impossible for Wolfe to fuel the fire with blowdown and ground litter. He made do by using his folding Swedish saw to cut down small aspen and cut them into segments. Soon, however, he exhausted that supply of wood and had to range further afield in order to find wood.

By then he was wearing virtually every garment he owned and still was cold as soon as he left the relative comfort of the lean-to and the fire.

"Dog, you and me got to do something about this. The problem is that I don't know how long it takes for a broken bone to knit. For now I'm gimping along on my knees while you run and play, darn you."

The dog came to him and nuzzled his side. Wolfe smiled and scratched behind its ears.

CHAPTER TWENTY-NINE

The first snowfall was little more than a skiff that barely covered the ground. But it was a harbinger of what was to come.

It had been Wolfe's intention to be far to the south and into a lower elevation before winter set in, but the broken leg made that impossible. As it was he had no choice but to make do as best he could, where he could.

"Dog, you're lucky you got all that fur to keep you warm. Now lie down. Stay. I got to find us some more meat lest we starve before spring lets us walk out of here. Darn leg should be healed by then; wouldn't you think? You agree? Good. Now stay put. I won't be long."

He collected, butchered, cut and dried the meat from two elk and one bear, saving their pelts. The skins were not properly tanned, but they would serve until the weather warmed and that was all he asked of them.

The bear skin, once it had been rough-cured and all the fleas had left, served as a bed, while the elk skins he carefully cut and sewed with elk skin thongs to make a cape that did well enough to protect him when he was away from the warmth of the lean-to.

He collected rocks and piled them in a low wall to act as a heat reflector.

Wolfe was surprised at how warm he could stay in the coldest of temperatures beyond the lean-to.

The dog helped, curling up next to him when they slept during the days and alerting him whenever game was coming down the hillside.

They had meat to eat, and that sustained them. But Wolfe would have killed for a hamburger and fries.

Wolfe judged it had been about two months before he felt up to trusting his leg to carry any weight, and by then the hills to the south were deep in snow. They were stuck where they were until the spring thaw.

CHAPTER THIRTY

They ran out of meat late that winter. The elk stopped coming down the hills, apparently having moved elsewhere. The deer disappeared as well, and the bears went into hibernation. Even the rabbits and squirrels holed up somewhere out of sight.

Wolfe and the dog were reduced to eating the odd sparrow that Wolfe could bring down with the blowgun. And those had become rare as well. Eventually he realized they would either move. Or starve.

The snow remained deep to the point of being nearly impassable, so Wolfe fashioned a pair of crude snowshoes made from young aspen growth tied together with thongs cut from a deerskin. There was nothing he could do to help the dog struggle across the drifts other than to sympathize.

Wolfe continued to worry about his leg strength but it was something he would just have to risk in order to move.

He packed his backpack, donned his elk skin cape and strapped on the backpack over it. Carrying his rifle, he and the dog set off, again moving as directly as possible toward the south and what should be warmer weather.

CHAPTER THIRTY-ONE

On the fourth day away from the comforts of the lean-to they were crossing a broad basin high in the mountains. Wolfe was unconsciously seeking familiar territory. There probably would have been an easier route to walk but this one he had driven several times in his truck. He could not remember the name of the basin, but the highway and the surrounding hills were familiar.

"What?"

The dog had stiffened into a stance that resembled a bird dog's point.

Wolfe peered in the direction the dog was looking. He saw a flicker of movement. And then another. Closer inspection proved the movement to be that of an ear.

Wolfe smiled as he raised the rifle and paused, waiting for the mule deer doe to step out from the brush that was hiding it. The rifle barked and eighty yards away the doe dropped, shot through the neck.

The dog raced ahead as Wolfe plowed through the snow to reach the doe and bleed it out. He had his knife out before he even reached his kill.

He made quick work of butchering the young mule, then carried the carcass to a stand of aspen where he cleared snow from a sizeable patch of ground and built a fire, piling wood on until he had a roaring blaze.

He slipped out of the backpack and brought out his trusty camp skillet that by now had seen a great deal of use. He put the skillet on the fire and scooped up snow to melt in it.

When he had a good amount of water he let the dog drink then returned the skillet to the fire and added more snow until he had more water. This time he allowed the water to heat.

The hot water tasted quite good, he thought, as good as any cup of coffee he had ever had.

When he had some coals to work with he allowed the active flame to subside while he layered strips of venison directly onto the coals. The dog did not wait for the niceties of cooked meat but gorged on the raw meat that Wolfe tossed it.

"Hello, who are you? Is that something cooking that I smell?"

Wolfe grabbed for his rifle and stood over the fire, ready to fight if that was what was offered.

CHAPTER THIRTY-TWO

A gaunt, red-haired man emerged from the trees. As far as Wolfe could see he was not armed. He wore a puffy, insulated coat that had seen better days and a Colorado Rockies baseball cap.

"Be all right if I come close, mister?" he called out.

Wolfe nodded. "Come ahead."

"Mister, I heard your rifle shot. It got my attention. There's only a few of us living up here, and we ran out of ammunition a long time ago. Haven't had much of anything to eat ever since then. That's why I came looking for you."

The man hesitated, his eyes cast down to the snow while he scraped his right foot back and forth. "The thing is…and I hate to do this, it goes against everything I always knew…but I come over here to beg. That's the blunt truth. I come begging from you, mister. A piece of meat, even the offal, anything you can spare because I got a sick woman and a kid and nothing to feed them."

"Nothing?" Wolfe said.

The man shook his head. "Not for almost a week now."

Wolfe glanced down toward his fire where strips of

venison were cooking, a thick aroma of searing meat and smoke rising from it.

The dog had already eaten, and there was more than enough for Wolfe, hungry though he was. He had intended to pack the excess with him, but….

"All right," he told the redhead. "Do you have anything to carry this in?"

CHAPTER THIRTY-THREE

"A few" folks was exactly what Wolfe found at the cabin where the red-head led him. There was the man, a woman lying under a mountain of blankets and a red-haired girl who looked to be about twelve years old.

From the state of things inside the cabin they had been living there before the nuclear conflagration that reshaped the country. When Wolfe arrived there was a blazing fire in a Franklin stove but even so the woman was shivering. The little girl was sitting at the woman's bedside trying to get her to take a drink of water that Wolfe assumed was melted snow.

"Mister, this is my wife, Harriet, and our daughter, Jennifer. My name is Miles, by the way. And you would be...?"

Wolfe introduced himself.

"What is your dog's name, Mr. Wolfe?" the child asked, showing some animation as she dropped to her knees to pet the dog and hug it.

"He, uh, he doesn't have a name. I've never gotten around to naming him," Wolfe said.

Jennifer looked first at the dog and then up at Wolfe. "His name is Buddy."

"You know that, do you?" Wolfe said with a smile.

The girl nodded, her expression quite serious. "I do."

"So it shall be then," Wolfe agreed.

While Wolfe was talking to the girl, Miles was busy getting the cooked venison onto plates – actual chinaware… and cloth napkins – that he tried to feed to his wife.

The woman was close to being unconscious and seemed uninterested in food, perhaps being beyond interest in food or in survival.

Jennifer was certainly hungry enough for both of them, rushing to eat but slipping tidbits of the venison to the dog – to the newly named Buddy – at the same time. Wolfe did not mind. Nor did Buddy,

"Under other circumstances, Mr. Wolfe, I would offer you some coffee, but…"

"Hot water will do just as nicely." Wolfe smiled. "I've come to actually enjoy it."

"Then hot water it shall be." Miles left his wife's side and put a kettle on the cast iron surface of the Franklin stove. "Will you stay the night with us, Mr. Wolfe? It would be nice to have company for a change."

It would be pleasant to have a night beneath a roof again, Wolfe thought. "I'd be pleased to, Miles."

"Jenny, make up a pallet for Mr. Wolfe, please."

"And one for Buddy, too, daddy?"

"All right. And one for Buddy, too."

CHAPTER THIRTY-FOUR

Wolfe woke early. The others were sleeping, Miles and the girl breathing softly but Harriet's breath ragged and harsh. She sounded bad.

He got up and made a trip to the outhouse behind the cabin, a rare and pleasant opportunity after so many months apart from any semblance of civilization.

On his way back inside he brought a load of firewood that Miles had split and piled against the back wall. Wolfe slipped his goggles over his eyes and added wood to the coals in the Franklin stove. The wood caught and flared into a bright, warming flame.

The iron stove clanked when he closed the doors over the flame. The sound disturbed Miles who sat up, blinking and rubbing his eyes.

"'Mornin', Mr. Wolfe. Care for more of my special hot water?" Miles grinned. "Better for you than coffee, y'know."

"It would be my pleasure," Wolfe answered.

Miles crawled out of his bunk and set the kettle on the stove before he too went outside, presumably to the outhouse. When he returned, Wolfe asked, "Tell me something, Miles. Are there elk nearby?"

"Oh, yes. The thing is, come a snowy winter like this one, the passes close and they're pretty much trapped here in the basin. There's feed enough that they don't starve. They're usually about a mile from here or a little better."

"I was thinking," Wolfe said. "I could knock one down and help you haul the meat over here. That should help you folks get through the winter anyway."

"That's a fine thing for you to do for us, Mr. Wolfe. Thank you."

Wolfe nodded. "We'll do it then. Is there any of that venison left over from last night?"

"A little," Miles said.

"Let's give the ladies some breakfast, then you and me will go see if we can't bring down something tasty."

CHAPTER THIRTY-FIVE

Wolfe's rifle barked and seventy yards away a large, bull elk staggered. Wolfe fired again and the animal went down.

He turned to Miles, who had guided him to the stand of quakies where a herd of more than a dozen elk could be found. He smiled and said, "There's a good amount of meat for you, friend."

"Friend indeed, Mr. Wolfe. Thank you."

"You know, it would be all right if you were to call me Jim. No need to be formal." Wolfe reached down to scratch the dog's ears and only then remembered that his companion was back at the cabin being fawned over by Jennifer.

"All right. Jim it is. Now let's go butcher that elk and cool the meat while it's so fresh."

The two of them walked forward through the snow to reach the downed bull. Miles knelt beside it and expertly opened an artery in its throat. "We'll let it bleed out for a few minutes before we open it up and start cutting if that's all right with you, Jim."

Wolfe nodded and the two men wiped the snow from a fallen aspen trunk so they could sit and make small talk while the elk bled.

Finally they turned the bull onto its back and got out their knives.

CHAPTER THIRTY-SIX

Jennifer clapped her hands with delight when she saw the mountain of meat the elk provided. "Can I have some right away?" she asked. "I want to make a broth for mama."

"Of course," Miles and Wolfe both said at virtually the same time. Jennifer laughed and quickly selected some choice bits and put them on the stove in a pot of water. The rest the men packed in snow in a washtub.

Jennifer sliced steaks for her father and Wolfe and a smaller piece for herself and put those in a skillet with some back fat to sizzle.

"Do you do all the cooking?" Wolfe asked the child.

She nodded. "I know how."

"She's good at it," Miles said. "Ever since her mother… well…you know." He paused, then brightened. "Say, do you know how to play acey-deucey?" Laughing, he added, "I can't play with Jen any more. She always beats me."

"I don't know the game," Wolfe said, "but I'm willing to learn."

They spent the rest of the afternoon and into the evening gorging on elk steaks and playing acey-deucey. And Miles was right. Whenever it was Jennifer's turn to play, she won handily.

CHAPTER THIRTY-SEVEN

"Good morning, Miles." Wolfe yawned and sat up, stretching and yawning some more.

"Good morning, Jim."

"I was thinking last night. Do you think you have enough meat to get you through or should we knock down another one before I head south?"

"Another wouldn't hurt," Miles said. "But you intend to move on? I was hoping you would stick around. If nothing else, you could teach me how to use that blowgun. One of those would come in handy come springtime. I bet you could take all sorts of small game with one."

"You could. And I'll teach you, but I can't stay much longer. I want to get home, Miles. Surely you understand that."

"Of course I do. Just a minute here. I'll wake Jennifer. She can cook us some breakfast."

"Let her sleep, Miles." Wolfe smiled. "A growing girl needs her rest."

"If you say so. I'll stir up those coals and get a fire going so we can burn our own steaks."

"Fair enough." Wolfe motioned to the dog and crawled to his feet. "If you would excuse us…" He and the dog – he kept forgetting that it was Buddy now – went outside for their morning relief.

Wolfe was only halfway through his morning needs when he heard a heart-wrenching scream from inside the cabin.

CHAPTER THIRTY-EIGHT

Wolfe raced inside to find Miles on his knees with Harriet cradled to his chest. Jennifer was at the bottom of the bunk, draped over her mother's legs. She and Miles were both sobbing.

Miles looked up at Wolfe, tears and snot running. He said, "She's gone, Jim. She was my life and now she's gone."

"Oh, Lord, Miles, I am so very sorry," Wolfe said.

At the moment he was not sure what he should do. He was, after all, the stranger here. He had not really known Harriet and now never would.

He did know Miles and Jennifer, though, and he liked them very much. There surely could be something he could do for them. Food was one thing that came to mind. There was meat in the house. He built up the fire and set a skillet on top of the stove then went out to the shed and sliced some steaks off the haunch that was hanging there in the cold.

He sliced away some bits and pieces as well and once inside dumped those into a pot along with enough snow to cover the meat once the heat melted the snow. In addition to the steaks he was cooking he wanted to make some broth. He suspected Miles and Jennifer would be more likely to take broth than to properly eat.

Wolfe fed Buddy and then took the dog outside so the two of them could finish the business that Miles' cries had interrupted.

He found a shovel in the shed and made a few stabs at the ground with it, but the soil was rock hard and would remain that way until spring. He suspected that digging a grave right now would be difficult in the extreme.

They could build a bonfire, he supposed and burn it until the ground beneath it was thawed enough to allow them to dig a proper grave for Harriet. He would talk about that with Miles when the man seemed ready to discuss such arrangements for his wife. But that would come later. For the moment he wanted to get the family to at least drink some hot broth.

"C'mon, Buddy, Let's go in and see can we offer some comfort."

CHAPTER THIRTY-NINE

Miles would accept neither meat nor broth; Jennifer took both and ate with the gusto of the growing child that she was, Wolfe was delighted to see the girl get something hot into her stomach. And Buddy benefitted from the steak that Miles rejected.

After breakfast, Wolfe tried again to separate Miles from his dead wife's body.

"This isn't healthy, Miles," Wolfe said, tugging at Miles' arm to no avail. "At least move back a bit so I can cover her for you."

Miles swung around so quickly that Wolfe thought the smaller man was attacking him. "You leave Harriet the hell alone. You don't know her. You got no business messing with my beautiful darlin'," Miles snapped.

Wolfe backed away from the grieving man and turned to Jennifer. She was on the floor, on her knees, hugging Buddy and softly crying, her face pressed into Buddy's fur, her tears lost against the big dog.

There seemed little Wolfe could do to help so he did the

best he could, going out to collect more snow to melt and more bits of elk to cook into a rich broth.

When he returned and the new batch of broth was cooking he sat and drank the mug of broth originally intended for Miles, who was still cradling Harriet in his arms, his face pressed to her bosom, the man's body shaking in spasms of grief.

If they could just get through this first day, Wolfe thought, perhaps he could get Miles interested again in the needs of the world around him.

CHAPTER FORTY

They bedded down early, each silent with his own thoughts. Buddy, he noticed, curled up tight against Jennifer. That was fine by Wolfe; the little girl needed some comfort.

He stoked the fire again and pulled his borrowed blanket high under his chin. He could hear someone sobbing but whether that was Jennifer or her father he could not tell.

Wolfe slept fitfully and sometime in the night woke to a chill in the room. He got up and added wood to the fire. He stood beside the stove until he was warmed through and heat was returning to the place. When he turned to go back to his pallet he saw that Miles was not in the bed beside Harriet's body.

That explained the cold temperature, Wolfe thought. Miles had gotten up and went outside, probably to answer a call of nature after being so long on his knees. His leaving allowed the cold, night air to invade the cabin.

That was good, Wolfe thought. Any separation from Harriet's body was a good thing for Miles, no matter how small it might be. The man needed to return to some semblance of the ordinary, and if a trip to the outhouse was the best he could manage that would just have to be enough.

Wolfe lay awake for a few minutes thinking he really needed to resume his march south. But this was no time to leave Jennifer and Miles. The two were not coping well with the loss of wife and mother. They needed someone to help tend to their needs and to the routine chores until they were ready to resume their lives without Harriet.

And what were they supposed to do with the body, Wolfe pondered. Burn all their available firewood or let the body freeze and bury her when the ground thawed?

Wolfe had no idea if the family had suffered past losses or if there might already be an area set aside as a cemetery. He would have to ask Miles in the morning. Or Jennifer if Miles was still so distant. The man had been silent, other than his weeping, ever since his wife died.

That could wait until morning, however.

Wolfe rolled onto his side and let himself drift back into sleep.

CHAPTER FORTY-ONE

Miles' side of the bed was empty when Wolfe woke in the morning. He assumed the man was out doing chores of some sort and thought nothing of it.

Wolfe made a trip to the outhouse without seeing Miles and returned to the cabin where Jennifer was beginning to stir, her hair tousled and tangled and down in her eyes.

"Good morning, sunshine," Wolfe said with a grin. "Did you sleep well last night?"

"I did, sir."

"Y'know, Jen, you don't have to call me sir. Jim will do."

"Could we settle for Mr. Wolfe, sir? I don't think I'm ready to start calling grown-ups by their first names yet." Jennifer sat up and pushed the hair back from her face. She very modestly tugged her pajamas in place, not that she was showing anything.

"Mr. Wolfe will do just fine, Jen. Whatever is comfortable for you." Wolfe picked up an armful of wood from the pile, noting that he would need to bring more in soon. He opened the cast iron doors on the Franklin stove and carefully placed the billets of firewood inside. The fire caught and flared up quickly.

"Hungry?" he asked.

"Yes, sir. I could eat a horse," she said.

"Yes, and before things get back to normal…if they ever do…you may very well have to."

"Ugh!" Jennifer grimaced, her nose wrinkling when she did so.

"Oh, it isn't all that bad," Wolfe told her while he used a greasy rag to wipe the cooking surface on the stove.

"You've eaten horse meat?"

"I have. There was a restaurant in…it was one of the small towns in eastern Colorado, I can't remember which one. I was driving a truck through to someplace. Stopped there for lunch and they had horse meat on the menu. Buffalo too. I'd already tried buffalo. Liked it too. Anyway, I thought I'd give horse a try. It wasn't bad. A little grainy. Nothing special though."

"I still say ick."

"Lucky for you," Wolfe said, "we still have plenty of elk, and before I leave I'll shoot another for you. Two if your dad wants them."

"I like elk meat," Jennifer said. She stood and began the process of getting dressed, standing there in the open but managing to not show anything that she should not.

"I'm with you, kid." Wolfe dropped some fat into a skillet and set it on the stove. "We need more elk steaks. How big do you want me to cut it for you?"

"This big," she said, holding her hands a good two feet apart.

"Listen, if you will eat that much, I will cook it for you."

"Don't you dare." Jennifer giggled and went back to dressing.

Wolfe picked up a butcher knife, ran a sharpening stone

over it for a few licks and went out to the shed where the elk carcass hung.

"Oh, Lord!" he said when he entered the shed.

There was more than an elk carcass hanging there.

Miles hung from one of the meat hooks too, his neck encircled by a sturdy rope and an empty nail keg tipped over at his feet.

Miles' body had already cooled in the frigid, winter air, so Wolfe judged the man must have come out and killed himself fairly early the night before.

How could the son of a bitch have left his daughter like that, Wolfe asked himself, more annoyed with Miles than saddened.

And how was he supposed to tell Jennifer about it. Wolfe hung his head and said a short prayer over Miles and his inability to cope with the present instead of seeing that his daughter needed him. For that, Wolfe could never forgive the man. Although he could understand a grief so terrible that it darkened his soul, he would not leave a child by herself.

CHAPTER FORTY-TWO

When Wolfe returned to the cabin, Jennifer was standing with her back to the stove, brushing her hair with long, slow strokes and humming something under her breath.

Wolfe sat at the table and watched her for a moment. Jennifer noticed his interest and his sorrowful expression.

"Is something wrong?" She stopped brushing.

Wolfe pushed the other kitchen chair away from the table. "Come sit down, please, Jen."

The child's expression changed to show sudden alarm. "What is it, Mr. Wolfe?"

"Sit down, please." When she did so, perching on the edge of the chair, he said, "There is…a problem, Jen. No, a tragedy really. It's…."

"Is something wrong with daddy? Where is he, Mr. Wolfe? Has something happened to him? He's always here when I wake up, but this morning…where is he, Mr. Wolfe?"

If he thought he could get away with a plausible lie, he would have told one. If Jennifer had been a few years younger, he could have lied to her and been believed. But the child was half grown and smart. And there would be no way to hide the truth.

Wolfe took a deep breath, took Jennifer's hands in his own and began talking.

CHAPTER FORTY-THREE

The girl broke into a torrent of tears. It was to be expected. First her mother and now her dad too. Wolfe ached for the child, but there was no comfort he – or anyone – could give that would assuage the pain of those losses coming one right after the other.

Frustrated and feeling helpless, Wolfe left Jennifer to her sorrow and went out to the shed where Miles' body hung.

He cut the body down and did what he could – it was not much – to arrange the dead man's face into a normal appearance. The act of hanging had left Miles' face disfigured. And Wolfe did not want the man's daughter to see him like that.

There was nothing he could do about the discoloration, though.

Bad as Miles looked when Wolfe was done with him, he had looked even worse, almost like a Halloween mask of himself, when Wolfe started.

Finally, unable to put the unenviable task off any longer, Wolfe picked Miles up and carried him inside, miserable about the task but grateful for the heat that radiated from the Franklin stove.

He carried Miles to the bed he had shared with Harriet and placed the body down gently beside that of his wife. Wolfe immediately tried to pull the covers up over Miles, but Jennifer stopped him.

"Wait, Mr. Wolfe. I want to see."

It was not a request Wolfe could deny. He nodded and stepped back away from the crudely built bed containing the bodies of the two people Jennifer loved most in this world.

"I'll leave you alone for a while," he mumbled. Motioning for Buddy to follow, he went back outside and busied himself splitting the wood that Miles had sawed and piled but had not gotten around to final stage of making it kindling and fit for the woodburner.

CHAPTER FORTY-FOUR

Wolfe cooked a big breakfast and insisted Jennifer eat some of it. She did so, but without appetite or enthusiasm. When they were done Wolfe moved his chair so he sat facing her. He leaned forward and took her hands in his.

"This is lousy, kid, but there's no help for it. Things are what they are, and we have to live with them. I'm sorry about your parents, but it is what it is. Do you have family some-where? Anywhere?"

Jennifer was crying again. Or still. Wolfe almost felt like it himself. She was just a child, and she had been dealt a truly lousy hand.

"Anywhere?" he repeated.

Jennifer shook her head.

"Nobody?"

Another shake.

Wolfe sighed. "The thing is, Jen, we can't stay here, and I can't leave you here by yourself. Wherever I go, I need to take you with me."

"Why?"

"Because I don't live here, Jen. My home is in Florida, and I'm trying to get back there to my family. I…I have to believe that they are still alive, that they are there waiting for me to come and get them. So that's what I am doing. And now it looks like you'll be doing it with me. You and Buddy."

He hoped the mention of the dog would encourage Jennifer. Buddy had been by her side pretty much the whole day, sitting close or even leaning against her leg. Wolfe believed the dog could sense Jennifer's pain and wanted to ease it as best he could.

"Florida. That's an awful long way from here."

"Yes, it is, Jen. I've been thinking…you might not like this, but it's the best I can think of…the ground is too hard to dig a grave for your folks, and I won't just close the door and walk away from them. The thing is, you should know what I intend to do. If you have objections, you have to say so. Now and at any time in the future. We can talk about anything you want. I'm the grown-up. I will decide. But I want you to tell me what you think about things. Okay?"

She almost managed a smile. "Okay, Mr. Wolfe. But…you say we have to leave?"

"Yes. We can't stay here. We'll pack up and move on first thing in the morning. Do you have a backpack? Like for school or something?"

She nodded.

"All right then. I want you to pack it with a few extra clothes. Nothing too heavy. Whatever you take, and it can't be much, you'll have to carry for something like two thousand miles. All right?"

The girl nodded again.

Wolfe patted her hands. "Make your choices. If you want to carry something to remember home by, that will be okay. Just remember that you'll be carrying it on your back for two thousand miles."

He got up and poured a cup of herb tea for himself and another for Jennifer. Buddy pressed himself against Jennifer's leg and whined very softly.

Off to the side of the room, the two bodies lay as if for a wake.

CHAPTER FORTY-FIVE

Wolfe woke early, as was his habit. Jennifer was already awake. He wondered if she had been able to sleep at all during the night. The girl's emotions were hers to wrestle and hopefully come to grips with. He would do his best, taking care of her as he could until he found a better home for her than he could offer as a man wandering the roads and a fugitive from misplaced justice.

She sat on the edge of her bed, peering down at the floor, eyes unfocused and blank.

"Are you all right?" he asked.

She nodded mutely.

"Ready to go?"

Jennifer waved a hand in the general direction of her backpack, which sat at the foot of her bed. It appeared to be plump and fully packed. "Do you want to look in it?" she asked without enthusiasm.

"No. You have to live with whatever you have there. That's entirely up to you, Jen."

"Do you want me to cook breakfast for us?" she asked, surprising him.

Wolfe started to tell her that he was used to cooking and would do it. Then it occurred to him that it might be good for her to have some work to do to take her mind off her dead parents, still lying beneath a quilt in the room with them.

"That would be nice, thank you," he said.

"What would you like, Mr. Wolfe?"

"What I would like? Three eggs. Poached. With toast and bacon." He smiled. "But I think I'll have an elk steak instead."

Wolfe built the fire up while Jennifer cut their meat and put it in the skillet with a dollop of fat. Later, after they ate, Wolfe asked, "Are you all right with what I said yesterday?"

"About…?"

"The house. And your, um, parents."

She nodded. "I thought about it a lot. You're right. It's the best thing to do."

"All right then, Jen. Get your backpack. I think we're ready to leave."

Jennifer was crying again but so very quietly that he had not noticed.

"You go ahead then. I'll join you in a moment," he said.

She crossed the room to her parents' bed, bent down and pulled the quilt back so she could kiss each one of them gently on the forehead. Then she stood, turned and walked resolutely out the door.

Wolfe did what had to be done inside then joined her by the shed.

CHAPTER FORTY-SIX

He took hold of Jennifer's hand and stood with her for a moment, the heat from the blaze warming their faces and hands while their backs remained cold in the chill morning air.

The house caught quickly, the weathered logs – cut and placed by Miles years before – dry and easily flammable. Within minutes it was fully engulfed, flames rising at least thirty feet.

Wolfe was surprised at how little smoke the aged-dried logs gave off. That would come later, he thought, when the fire began to consume the bedding and other articles inside.

It was fairly noisy, the fire crackling and popping to the point that he feared he might have left some live cartridges inside.

He also feared that Jennifer would decide to rush in at the last moment, to give her parents another goodbye or to retrieve something she had forgotten. Instead she stood, mute and stone-faced while everything she had ever known – and everyone – went up in flames.

Tears and snot ran down the little girl's face. She made no effort to wipe them away nor did she try to hide them.

After several minutes, when the flames burned their highest, Jennifer turned to Wolfe. "All right, Mr. Wolfe. I'm ready to go now."

He again took her by the hand and led her away. Toward the south.

CHAPTER FORTY-SEVEN

Wolfe stopped at the concrete strip that had been US 50. He stood there for a moment, then began to laugh.

"Mr. Wolfe? What is it, sir?" Jennifer asked, looking more than a little nervous to be in the custody of a grown-up who she barely knew.

"Me, Jen. I'm laughing at myself. Do you know what I just did?"

"No, sir."

"I stopped and looked both ways. Didn't want to be run over by passing traffic." He laughed again. "Force of long habit, although I don't suppose there has been a car or a truck on this road in the past couple years." He looked down at the girl. "Being raised up in the mountains where there wasn't so much traffic anyway I don't suppose you were taught that quite so strongly."

"No, sir. I was always able to hear if there was something on the road." She smiled. "But I looked out for bears and snakes and stuff the way you look out for cars."

Wolfe motioned for her to follow and stepped out onto

the pavement. "Come on, kiddo. Let's go see if there's anyone left in what used to be Canon City."

They followed the highway, already beginning to frost heave, past the road to Royal Gorge and down into the Arkansas River valley where Canon City lay.

And there Wolfe got the biggest surprise yet on his journey home.

CHAPTER FORTY-EIGHT

"Welcome, folks." The speaker was smiling and pleasant, holding his hand out to Wolfe to shake. "Welcome to Canon, the biggest little city in the Red Zone. My name is Charles. What are yours?"

Wolfe blinked. He was not accustomed to this sort of welcome. Not since the war turned his world upside-down.

He introduced Jennifer and himself and was pleased when Charles said, "We have a number of young people who should be about your age, Jennifer. You might enjoy getting to know some of them.

"And you, Jim. I see you're carrying a rifle and a bow. You would fit right in with our hunters." He smiled. "We've become a hunter-gatherer society, at least for the time being. In the meantime we're trying to grow grain crops close to the river.

"It's the river that sustains us. Once there was no more electricity to operate the well pumps, people naturally gravitated toward live water. And that we have in abundance. We are still trying to work out our irrigation needs. In the meantime we haul water with horse power and hand water our crops. But don't worry. It will all come together in due time."

"How many folks do you have here now?" Wolfe asked.

"Understand, now, we haven't taken a census to give an exact number, but I would think our population to be in the neighborhood of forty thousand."

"I'm amazed you can feed that many," Wolfe said.

"Oh, it is touch-and-go at times. And people come, stay a while, then wander on elsewhere. Ours is a very fluid population. Which is part of the reason our farming hasn't progressed any quicker than it has. We lack the consistent manpower that farming requires. But we make do. Hunting, fishing, everything going into a communal pot.

"You should understand that, Jim. There is no private property here. If you choose to stay, and I hope you will, you must agree to that condition. Otherwise we will wish you well but tell you good-bye. Do you understand that?"

Wolfe nodded. He understood. He was not so sure he wanted to stay for any length of time under those conditions. But he understood.

"Come now," Charles said. "You've been traveling. You must be hungry." He motioned for Wolfe and Jennifer to follow and led the way into town.

CHAPTER FORTY-NINE

Just as the good folks back in Baggs had, communal living here led to a local school cafeteria being pressed into service as the dining hall. Or in this case, due to the large population, several school cafeterias.

Wolfe and Jennifer were taken to what had been an elementary school and led inside to the kitchen and dining hall where they were given cups of an herbal tea – Lord knew what went into the stuff, but it tasted bitter but not too bad – and a steel tray with some soggy greens – dandelion? – and a piece of meat that looked like a chicken leg and thigh.

"It's rabbit," Charles said. "Technically speaking I suppose it is really hare, but we call it rabbit. We run strings of snare lines around our grain fields to keep the rabbits from coming in and eating all the sprouting young plants. Dual purpose, you see. Food for our people and crop protection too."

Charles waved away a woman who brought him tea. "Hot water for me, Margaret. Thank you." He settled into a chair across the table from Wolfe and Jennifer and said, "Jennifer, if you decide to stay here with the other young people, one of your jobs will probably be to walk a snare line first thing in the morning to collect any rabbits the snares have caught."

Judging by the expression on Jennifer's face, Wolfe suspected that would be a chore that was not to her liking. And he noticed she did not show much enthusiasm for the meat on her tray, preferring to concentrate instead on the greens.

Unlike his young companion, Wolfe thoroughly enjoyed the rabbit. It was good meat, clean and fine-grained. The drawback to eating rabbit was that the meat contained virtually no fat. A steady diet of rabbit would not sustain a body.

Buddy did not seem to mind it, though. Jennifer slipped her rabbit quarter to him. The big dog ate it bones and all.

"I hope you have no objection," Charles said, "but our transient quarters here are in the old territorial prison."

"Territorial?" Wolfe said.

Charles laughed. "Yes, it is that old. It was turned into a museum a long time ago and hadn't been in active service for I don't know how long."

"It's interesting," Jennifer said. "Our class took a tour there once upon a time."

"Everything else is pretty much filled," Charles said, "but if you decide to live here we'll try to find something better for you."

When they were done eating, Charles stood. He said, "Grab your things. I'll take you over to the prison and see if we can't get you a room...or a cell...to stay in tonight."

Once again Wolfe and Jennifer trailed along behind their host as he led them out of the school and up a tree shaded street.

CHAPTER FIFTY

The prison – or museum – was located at the western edge of town. An elderly man wearing a large nametag that said 'warden' led them to a rock walled cell.

"You don't have to worry about that door," he told them. "The lock hasn't worked in years. And if it did, I don't know where we would find the key. If you folks don't mind, I've put both you and your daughter in the same cell. It's not that we're so crowded, but I think a family should be together. Is that all right?"

"It's fine, thanks," Wolfe said. Jennifer remained silent.

When the warden had gone to tend to his duties, whatever they might have been, Wolfe and Jennifer both stripped off their backpacks and dropped them onto the double-decker bunks in the cold, musty cell.

"Top bunk for you, Jen," he said.

"Good. I like a top bunk." She sighed. "At home I used to wish I had a top bunk. And a little brother to sleep in it. Sometimes I would even pretend."

"It must have been lonely there," Wolfe offered.

"Oh, I didn't mind it," she said. Then gave him a half-hearted smile. "Most of the time."

"What do you think about Canon?" he asked.

"It seems nice. Except for the part about the rabbits. I mean, I know where meat comes from. But rabbits are so cute and soft and furry. I don't want to hurt them." She giggled. "I think if I had to walk that snare line I'd just turn loose any rabbits that I caught."

"And go hungry?"

She shrugged.

"I don't know about you," Wolfe said, "but I could use a nap." He experimented inside the cell with his goggles on and without them. There was just enough light in the cell to make the goggles necessary, even though he was more comfortable without them.

Jennifer climbed onto the top bunk and lay down. Wolfe stretched out in the bunk beneath hers. The mattress was thin and a little too hard, but compared with sleeping on the ground it was the height of comfort.

Buddy seemed comfortable enough on the stone floor, curling into a ball at the head of the bed.

"G'night, kiddo."

"It isn't night, Mr. Wolfe."

"Close enough for me. Now go to sleep."

CHAPTER FIFTY-ONE

Wolfe slept for only a few hours and woke up feeling refreshed but hungry. He guessed hunger was a normal condition here. No wonder they invited him to stay and become a community hunter.

He sat up and adjusted the goggles covering his eyes, then stood and looked at Jennifer. She was sleeping soundly and looked like she would stay that way for some time.

Wolfe motioned for Buddy to join him and quietly let himself out of the cell and on to the outside, pausing so Buddy could do his business on an overgrown bit of yard, then with the dog at his side walked into town.

The Arkansas River ran fast and deep through the town. Half a dozen or more men were on its banks fishing with cast nets but seldom with much success, at least none that he observed in the few minutes he stood there watching.

In town several buildings that had been stores were now put into service of another sort. Several were devoted to manufacturing, working mostly in wood. In one he was delighted to see a group of ladies making arrows. They even looked like good ones. Wolfe stepped inside.

Here the ladies were using wooden dowels for arrow shafts and pine tar to glue split feathers in place. Farther back in the large room, other women were cutting arrow heads out of the steel in old "tin" cans and sharpening them.

"What would I have to do to get some of these arrows?" he asked the nearest woman, a thin lady with gray hair and pale eyes. His own supply of arrows was dwindling. He had enough to almost fill his bow-mounted quiver with nothing in reserve.

"You hunt?" she asked.

"Yes, ma'am."

The woman inclined her head toward a barrel that sat near the front window. "Pick through those. Any of 'em looks good to you, mister, you're welcome to take them. Take as many as you like."

"What would they cost?" he asked.

She gave him a sharp look. "You must be new here."

"Yes, ma'am."

"We don't use money here. No point in it these days. It's all share and share alike." She paused to push her hair back off her face. "Like I said, mister. Take what you can use and welcome."

"Now that is an offer I can't pass up," Wolfe said with a smile. "Thank you."

He headed for that barrel, Buddy walking close at his side.

CHAPTER FIFTY-TWO

The arrows were not of uniform quality. Many of them had shafts that were too slender, too weak, for the power of his bow. A few, only a very few, were poorly made. He did, however, find some that he could use. He had two empty slots on his bow-mounted quiver. He took a pair of the best to fill those spots and selected an even dozen more to keep in reserve.

"Is this all right? I don't want to be greedy, but I like what you ladies are doing here," he told the gray-haired woman.

"I told you to take as many as you like," she said, smiling. "I meant it. You can see we have plenty stockpiled there."

"Thank you, ma'am."

Wolfe took his bundle of arrows and walked back to the prison. The bunk where Jennifer had been sleeping was empty so he sat on the edge of his bunk with the bow in his lap and his backpack on the floor by his feet. Buddy sat nearby.

Wolfe reached out and scratched the big dog behind the ears. "I didn't do much toward getting us something to eat, fella, but this is good stuff. Too good to pass up.

"I tell you what. We saw a lot of birds out there. Why don't I take the blowgun and knock us down a few."

Buddy wagged his tail and inched a little closer to Wolfe.

Wolfe filled his quiver and carefully put the rest of the arrows into his backpack. He did not want to damage the fletching on those arrows.

"Ready?" he said when he was done.

Buddy wagged some more.

Wolfe set the bow aside and collected his blowgun and darts, then headed outside and toward the river in his quest for a snack.

CHAPTER FIFTY-THREE

"Nine should be enough," Wolfe said while Buddy sat eagerly eyeing the pile of songbirds Wolfe had collected.

Wolfe took the birds upriver, mindful of the communal laws in Canon, until he was well away from the town.

He gathered some driftwood and used a magnifying glass to start a fire, preferring the glass to using any of the now precious gas in one of his butane lighters.

While the fire was burning itself down to coals, Wolfe cleaned the birds. He tossed the feathers onto the river. They floated with the current. He was amused to recall how diligently the men in Canon were throwing their cast nets – and producing nothing – while here a number of small trout rose to nibble at the discarded feathers.

Finally he found some longer sticks and used those to dangle the bird carcasses over the coals of his fire.

As soon as the birds were cooked – he could eat raw meat if he had to but certainly had no desire to do so – Wolfe tossed three of the birds to Buddy while he ate three himself.

"Share and share alike," he mumbled around a mouthful of stringy flesh.

When he and the dog had both consumed their share, Wolfe packed the remaining three birds into the bag where he carried his darts. He was fairly sure Jennifer would not be getting enough food here. These birds should help at least a little.

Wolfe sat for a while staring at the rushing, swirling river then he stood and brushed himself off.

It was time to go back to town and soon to move on south. Jennifer could decide for herself if she wanted to stay here where there were other young people or walk on with him.

He glanced down at Buddy as it occurred to him that Jennifer might want to keep the dog with her. She had become extremely fond of Buddy. It surprised him that he felt a pang of loss when he thought the dog might stay with the girl. It seemed he was more attached to Buddy than he had realized.

Even so, that would be Jennifer's call. The child had lost enough and more than enough when she lost her parents and her home and virtually all her worldly possessions. Wolfe did not want to take Buddy away from her too.

"We'll just have to see, won't we," he said aloud. Buddy's ears pricked up at the sound. Wolfe bent down while walking and ruffled the dog's head and ears.

CHAPTER FIFTY-FOUR

Wolfe waited in their cell but Jennifer did not show up. Eventually the old warden came by and said, "Supper time, mister. You don't want to miss that."

"No, I certainly don't. Thanks for reminding me."

"You're welcome." He laughed. "It's all part of my official duties."

The warden walked on – to perform more of his official duties, Wolfe supposed – while Wolfe stood and stretched. He stashed Jennifer's three roasted birds beneath the pillow on her bunk, patted his thigh as a signal to Buddy to follow and headed for the chow hall.

Jennifer was already there. She smiled when she saw Wolfe. And Buddy.

"What have you been up to?" Wolfe asked while Jennifer was busy petting Buddy.

"I've been having fun. This afternoon I took a class in finding edible plants. And a lady in the garment factory started teaching me how to sew. And I made three new friends. Mr. Wolfe, I would like you to meet Tanya and Roberta and Billie."

The girls were all about Jennifer's age. They seemed polite and pleasant, good company for the child.

"You like it here, do you?" he said.

Jennifer nodded vigorously. "I do. A lot."

"That's great," he said. He meant it. It would be good if Jennifer could grow up in a happy environment.

Wolfe went to the serving line to collect his supper, which turned out to be a soup of some sort of broth – perhaps it was better not to know the origin – with a handful of bitter greens floating in it.

The taste was not much, but it was hot and filled the void in his belly.

Wolfe was almost done with his meal when a stocky man with streaks of gray beginning to show in his beard approached.

"Pardon me, mister, but I have to take the dog now."

Wolfe carefully placed his spoon in his soup bowl then turned to face the man. "Why would you do a thing like that?"

"It's the rules, mister. We don't have food enough for ourselves. We sure can't afford to waste any of it on pets. The dog has to go."

"And by 'go' you mean exactly what?" Wolfe asked, his tone of voice deceptively mild.

"The animal is meat, mister. He'll go into the pot and help us all. Good thing too. He looks like he has a good bit of meat on those bones."

The man reached for Buddy's collar.

CHAPTER FIFTY-FIVE

Two burly men stepped up behind Wolfe and quietly took him by the arms while the first man reached down and gripped Buddy by the scruff of his neck.

Wolfe and the dog reacted at virtually the same moment. And with the same object in mind.

Wolfe jerked forward, throwing the man holding his right arm across the dining table, through a young couple's meal and into their laps while the man on his left was flung off his feet and several yards out onto the floor where he hit with a thud and a shout of surprise.

Buddy, meanwhile, had turned in the stocky man's grip and had his teeth sunk into the fellow's wrist.

Wolfe lashed out with the edge of his hand, chopping down hard on the man's forearm. He heard the dull snap of a bone breaking, and the man screamed, his voice high pitched and shrill.

"Dog!" Wolfe barked and patted his thigh to signal Buddy to him.

The big dog released his victim, blood streaming down his hand and dripping onto the floor. He came to Wolfe's side and obediently sat although he was quivering with the desire to strike out again.

"Anyone touches my dog will get the same," Wolfe warned.

Without a backward glance, he and the dog stalked out of the mess hall and back to their quarters in the old prison.

His backpack was still packed and ready. All he had to do was pick it up and strap it on. Wolfe was just reaching for it when Jennifer came running in, tears streaming down her cheeks.

"They were going to eat Buddy."

"Yes," Wolfe said, "they were."

"That's awful, Mr. Wolfe."

Wolfe smiled and patted the girl's shoulder. "To you and me it is though I can understand their point of view. Anyway, that's behind us now. Buddy and me are leaving."

"Now?"

He nodded. "Right now, kiddo. There's no point in waiting, and the quicker I get out of here the better."

"I'm coming with you, Mr. Wolfe."

"I thought you liked it here," he said.

"Not now I don't. Not when they eat dogs here. I'm coming with you." She picked up her much smaller backpack and slung it on. "Please?"

The three of them walked out, past the self-appointed warden and a delegation of local men who were coming after either Wolfe or Buddy – he did not bother to ask them what they wanted, just brushed past them.

They crossed a bridge over the Arkansas and headed into the night. Water was life and the Arkansas was flowing with all they needed. "Follow 50 and follow the river. Every step is one step closer to home," Wolfe said as much to himself as to the girl walking with him, her hand knotted up in the heavy fur of the big dog.

CHAPTER FIFTY-SIX

"I'm glad to be free of those people, Mister Wolfe."

"Forty thousand in one town? They are too big to survive," Wolfe pondered. "If they have to eat dogs, then they're too far gone to make peace with."

Wolfe was thinking about everything he had heard when he was there. Control. Common good. Living in a jail. People coming and going like birds at a feeder.

When people wanted to stay, that is the group that would be able to look after Jennifer. But if she stayed behind, Buddy would probably stay with her. He liked that dog even if the beast never told him someone was sneaking up on them while they were sleeping. He wondered what a good night's sleep looked like. Then again, there was no need to waste time thinking about that kind of stuff. It didn't help anyone.

Jennifer hummed as she walked, a tune that children devised when they were happy. On occasion, she would skip. The dog walked beside her, the two growing inseparable. Was he ready to raise a twelve-year old?

All because he did not want to leave the dog behind?

The road wound along the river or maybe it was the river

that followed the road. They passed people, but did not stop to talk. Wolfe always nodded politely. They were more wary of him, traveling armed with a rifle and a bow, but the young girl put them more at ease.

Would FEDCOM see him as James Wolfe, the outlaw and his killer dog or would they look right past a man with brown hair traveling with a young girl who kept a dog as a pet? He had two sets of hair dye left. Would that be enough to keep his hair the color that would get him past the Clear Areas?

The next couple they happened across, Wolfe stopped and waved. They had a shanty down by the water that they were fishing from. A small tendril of smoke told of a fire probably used for cooking. It didn't seem to throw off much heat outside of the burning tinder.

"Can you tell us how far to the Clear Area?"

An old man waved indiscriminately. An old woman, maybe his wife, punched him in the arm and that started an argument. His cane pole bent with a bite and that instantly turned the pair from brawlers to lovers. They focused completely on bringing the fish to shore. The old woman waded into the water where she could use a pair of sticks like a scoop. The old man brought the fish close enough. The woman drove the sticks into the water and with a quick flick of the wrist, the fish was flying toward the shore where the old man pounced like a cat, landing on all fours to keep their prize from escaping. He brained the fish on a rock.

The two cheered like kids at a football game.

Wolfe and Jennifer waited to get their attention again. Wolfe cleared his throat so the old couple would remember they had guests.

"Who are you?" the man shouted in surprise.

"James Wolfe, sir, at your service. I asked how far the

Clear Area is and if you could point us in that direction, please."

The man looked back to his fish, produced a disgraceful looking knife, and started to clean his catch. The woman wiped her hands on her apron, looking fresh from a farmhouse instead of a shack along a river with nothing to her name.

She pointed in the direction they were heading. "Two days' walk. You can't miss it."

"Much obliged, ma'am. Enjoy your lunch." Wolfe beat feet out of there. Jennifer ran-walked to keep up. The big dog trotted happily. The sun was up and warming the air but it was still cool, perfect for covering ground. He figured the old woman's two days was a day at his pace.

Jennifer didn't complain, but when he looked back, he found she was breathing hard and her face red from her efforts. He slowed. If it took two days, it took two days. He had a long way to go, but was finally making progress.

CHAPTER FIFTY-SEVEN

Wolfe heard something. He was in the middle of another short bout of sleep when the sound penetrated his sleep. The big dog growled louder and louder. With Jennifer, Wolfe was sleeping at night without his goggles. It was more comfortable that way. On the other side of the dog, the girl was fast asleep.

He followed the dog's eyes to see what was upsetting the big animal, expecting to see men with guns pointed at him, but they weren't there. He could see perfectly fine in the dark and did not see anything at all, but he trusted Buddy. He growled for a reason, even if that reason was that men were already there and pointing guns.

Wolfe rose and looked around. He pulled the AR15 from beneath his sleeping bag and pointed the business end where the dog was looking. "Stay," he whispered pointing at Jennifer. The dog cocked its head. "Just stay there and protect her. I'll be right back."

He didn't know if the dog would get it or not, but the animal was plenty smart, plus he was more attached to her than Wolfe. He trusted that and turned his attention back to the brush beyond their rough campsite.

He took two more steps before the outline of a massive beast of a mountain lion materialized beyond the first bush. Wolfe stopped and took aim.

"I can see you, unlike most of your prey, I suspect. It'd be best for both of us if you turned tail and headed for the hills. There's nothing for you down here." Wolfe kicked sideways at the coals of the fire hoping to spark something to life, bring fear to a creature that generally knew none.

The mountain lion froze in its tracks. A good two hundred pounds or more. It was king of the Red Zone jungle, or Wolfe didn't know his kings.

"That's a good boy. Go on." The big cat stopped listening and crouched, its back legs dancing as it prepared to attack.

Wolfe didn't want to kill something if he wasn't going to eat it. He launched himself like a missile at the cat, catching it right as it jumped. He powered an uppercut into its chin sending the cat high into the air. It landed to the side of the fire. Wolfe jumped over it to get between it and Jennifer, but the big cat had had enough. It bounded away as fast as its legs could carry it.

Buddy finally stopped growling. He had not left the youngster's side. Now with the threat gone, he laid back down and closed his eyes. Jennifer never awoke.

When they got up the next morning, Wolfe slid his goggles into place. He didn't bother telling her about the mountain lion. He didn't want her to lose sleep over it. She probably wouldn't because they walked so far during the day that she would be tired. Hell, He was tired and she was taking twice as many steps as he was.

CHAPTER FIFTY-EIGHT

The old woman had been right. Two days passed as two days would. After a great deal of walking, they spotted the checkpoint up ahead. Wolfe's first instinct was to dive off the road and circle around it, but with his brown hair and the young girl, he didn't look like the man on the wanted posters. If they waited until nightfall, then he could hide the welding goggles, too, squinting his way past the checkpoint lights before they crossed.

Except he wouldn't be able to explain the rifle. He'd exchanged the M16 for an AR15 back outside Canon City. Still, he was worried about going through the checkpoint with it and half a satchel of ammunition. He expected they would confiscate most if not all of it.

Confiscate. A gentleman's word for steal.

Wolfe wanted to trust people. It was in his nature to be gracious and that had gotten him into too much trouble in this new world. Trying to help when it would have been best to go the other way. His life would have been much easier if he had.

Even with the radiation from the nuclear bombs, mirrors

still existed. When he looked into them, he had to be comfortable with the man who looked back. They'd wait and go through the checkpoint. He'd try to keep all of his stuff with him, but if they took it, he would make do. He had before and he would again.

If they messed with Jennifer or the dog, then there would be a fight.

He hoped they wouldn't. He wanted to believe in a world where one man trusted another.

"We'll rest here and go through the checkpoint after dark."

"As you wish, Mister Wolfe. Do you want me to cook our dinner?"

"Sure, Miss Jennifer. I think I heard a couple rabbits scruffling around on the ground not far from here. You and Buddy get the fire ready. We'll start it when I get back."

Jennifer held onto the scruff of Buddy's neck and nodded.

Wolfe left all his worldly possessions on the ground by her and walked away carrying just his bow and some of the new arrows from Canon City. He had a few of the original broadheads left and those were gold in case he needed to use them against something special.

Say a mountain lion, for example.

Wolfe stalked his prey and found them easily enough. Not rabbits but prairie dogs. They'd probably be a bit tough, but something was better than nothing. He took careful aim, pulled, and released, sending the new arrow true to its target. He quickly nocked a second arrow, counting on his unnatural speed to help him take two shots where a normal man would only get one.

The second arrow pinned the prairie dog into the mouth of the hole, head half underground. Wolfe smiled at the skill of the second shot. He remembered when he first acquired the bow. It was not that long ago. Practice and need had driven him to learn it and do better.

He looped his bow over his head and through one arm so he could pull out his knife. With the first cut, a terrible cry shook the ground.

Wolfe looked up in time to see the mountain lion leaping. He drove the knife upward with his inhuman strength, through the cat's breastbone and through its heart. The two-hundred pounder hit him head high. He fell over backwards, hitting the ground with a thump. He threw the great cat from him and jumped to his feet, ready to keep fighting, but it was dead.

"You'll make a nice jacket," he told the cat. "But not a good dinner."

He finished cleaning the prairie dogs before skinning the mountain lion and cutting off its head. Jennifer wouldn't like it, but he needed the brains if he was to do a proper job tanning the hide.

CHAPTER FIFTY-NINE

"We need to wait another day so I can get this hide tanned enough that it won't rot on us before we get where we have to go."

Jennifer shrugged. "I don't have anywhere to be, Mister Wolfe."

"I wanted to talk about that." He kept his eyes on his work, cleaning the blood and meat from the underside of the mountain lion's pelt. He used his knife as a scraper as well as a sharpened rock. "What do you want out of your life? I mean, what do you want to do when you grow up?"

"What does anyone want to do?" she replied, sounding like an adult trapped in a twelve-year old's body. "I hope that I can find someone and be together like my Ma and Pa were. They were happy. See, with us, before the bombs and after the bombs were about the same. I didn't go to school out here. I was home-schooled. So nothing much changed besides we couldn't get any groceries, like sugar and flour."

"I miss bread," Wolfe said absentmindedly, thinking of the greasy truck stop burgers that always seemed to hit the spot.

A few of them had good fries, even. There is a trick to frying them that not many mastered.

"I don't know what I want to do besides help you make it to your family, if you'll let me tag along."

She kept up without complaint. If only he had a horse for them to ride, they'd get there in a third the time. But they didn't have a horse.

"Looks like it will just be the three of us," he shared, not dwelling on what they did not have.

"I'll cook those prairie dogs, but they aren't real dogs, are they?"

Wolfe laughed and shook his head. "I wouldn't eat a dog. A hot dog, maybe, but not someone like Buddy."

"I saw what you did to those men when they tried to take him."

Wolfe kept scraping and pulling the hide. He knew it would shrink with the tanning, but he had no way to keep it stretched.

"We don't need to think about those things. I won't let anything happen to Buddy. Not if I can help it anyway."

"Or me?"

"Or you."

"I have nowhere to go." She looked at him as she worked their one frying pan over the fire, trying to get the greasy prairie dog meat to cook evenly. It sizzled as it slid back and forth across the pan. "If you'll have me, I'll stay with you and Buddy until you make it to see your Lurleen and JoJo. Tell me about JoJo."

Wolfe smiled even though a tear welled into his eye. It had been so long that the memories of his family were starting to fade. He could hear the little boy's laughter. He could hear Lurleen running after him.

"I spent all my time on the road so they could have a better life. Driving is something that I am good at. I was good at." He pointed at his boots with the knife in his hand. "I missed out on a lot of his first two years. I was not there when the bombs fell."

He took a break from scraping the hide. Why was he baring his soul to a twelve-year old?

"Sure, Miss Jennifer. I'll adopt you and keep you safe. I think you'll like my Lurleen." Jim Wolfe spent the rest of the afternoon and evening talking about the one person that mattered most to him. The more he talked, the more she came back to life. And little JoJo. He could almost see him.

The young girl would be a nice addition to his family. And Buddy, too.

"One more day working this hide and tomorrow night, we'll pass the checkpoint."

Wolfe disappeared into his own thoughts, wondering about many things. Had the mountain lion tracked them through the day? It looked like the same beast. How was he going to get through the checkpoint?

He would improve his chances by taking a look after it was nice and dark.

CHAPTER SIXTY

Wolfe slowly stuck his head over the top of a small dirt rise. The checkpoint was not more than a hundred yards away. It consisted of a small building with concrete blocks in front of it, as if someone was going to drive a semi into the building. He turned toward the Red Zone. Not a single light for as far as he could see.

He wondered if these were set up after the bombs, when the new FEDCOM thought the wilders would come from the wasteland driving cobbled together vehicles sporting machineguns and flamethrowers. No one in the Red Zone had powered vehicles. A horse and buggy would not make much of a dent in their concrete.

Federal Command. Dictators worse than anything outside the Clear Area, a title that meant they were the sole authority. They were making Wolfe's life hell. All because of the corrupt Major Henkin and the damn Alston brothers. The most vile creatures borne from the radioactive ashes of the war.

Maybe it was different on this side of Colorado heading

toward Kansas. Maybe they hadn't gotten the alert. Maybe his new hair color would protect him.

He shook off his thoughts and studied the checkpoint. No one went through while he watched. Half the night he waited while the two soldiers did everything they could to keep themselves awake.

As he was getting ready to return to Jennifer and Buddy, he heard a truck's diesel engine revving in the distance. He waited and sure enough, the military truck came over a rise farther in the Clear Area. It approached without being in a hurry and stopped by the checkpoint. Two soldiers got out while the driver yelled something obscene from the cab, making everyone laugh. They stood in front of the headlights which gave Wolfe a chance to get closer. None of them wore the night vision goggles that seemed to be so plentiful back in Idaho.

Wolfe crouched and moved forward, sticking to the depressions between the rolling landscape. When he was only twenty yards beside the checkpoint, he ducked into a culvert and listened.

The four made small talk while the driver listened to music blasting out from the cab of the truck.

Little things that people took for granted. Waylon Jennings. Wolfe listened to the old classic. He liked it and let it make him feel good, like it used to.

After a few minutes, the two who had been standing guard waved and climbed into the back of the truck.

The first thing the two new guards did was make a fire and start an old-fashioned percolator coffee pot boiling. They sat around the fire without a care in the world, their M16 rifles slung forgotten over their backs. The pair continued joking as Wolfe disappeared back into the night.

CHAPTER SIXTY-ONE

Without a word, Jennifer packed her small back pack. Wolfe draped the mountain lion cloak over the pack and her in case it started to rain. The dry of eastern Colorado could benefit. The river ran steady, but was lower than usual, if the marks on the shore were anything to go by.

Night had settled and the two stepped onto the road. Jennifer stayed close, between Wolfe and Buddy because she couldn't see like the man or the dog.

Wolfe guided them forward, walked slowly but steadily. He wasn't in a hurry to his own funeral. There was no need to alarm the guards.

And every step was one step closer to Florida. "I think you'll like Florida, Miss Jennifer. It's nothing like here. We don't get any snow at all down there. Sun, sand, and bugs. Don't go too close to the swamps because of the snakes and alligators, but they are easy enough to avoid once you've learned a thing or two."

He spoke in a low voice, knowing that it would carry, to alert the guards that they were coming without being alarming.

"I look forward to it," Jennifer said and started to skip. Wolfe smiled to himself and steered her away from a pothole as they continued their journey down the middle of the highway 50.

Fifty yards from the checkpoint, the guards finally flipped a switch on a blindingly bright light. Wolfe fumbled for his welding goggles, pulling them over his face. He saw sunspots while his eyes felt like they had been burned by a torch.

He blinked quickly to clear the white and the pain while his eyes watered. He froze in place while Jennifer took one more step, stopping when he didn't come with her.

"Are you okay?" her voice was innocent with a hint of fear. He could sense her other hand tangled deep within Buddy's heavy neck hair.

"I will be fine. Let me get my night lights working again." His joke was lost on her. The gray haze that was what he saw of a bright world through his goggles started to appear. He blinked a few more times and started walking again. He waved his free arm.

"Ho!" he called, although he had already been seen. He did not know about the spotlight or the electricity to power it. His visit the previous night had not been complete.

The guards had their rifles in their arms and were pointing them at Wolfe and the girl.

"Don't get many visitors this way?" Wolfe asked. "We are just passing through, if that's alright, sir?"

"It's not alright. Stand up and be counted!" one guard yelled. The other snickered and slung his weapon.

"AC/DC! Nice one, Hank." The second guard motioned for Wolfe to put his arms in the air. Jennifer threw hers into the air, too, but when Buddy started to growl, she dropped her arms and wrapped them around the big dog's neck. She whispered into his oversized furry ear, and he stopped growling.

"Come closer where we can get a good look," the first guard ordered, the barrel of his rifle pointed at Wolfe's chest.

"We came here peaceful like. No need to point guns."

"What's that on your shoulder? Peaceful men don't carry an armory!" The second guard pointed at the bow and AR15 over Wolfe's shoulder.

"Have you been out there?" Wolfe pointed with his chin over his shoulder toward the soulless land behind him. "Only fools travel unarmed out there. Just yesterday we killed a mountain lion. It was him or us. Go on, Jennifer, show him your pelt."

The girl turned in a circle to show the guards.

"That's one big cat. He was out there? Less than a day away?"

"Yes, sir," Wolfe confirmed. He kept his breathing slow and steady. He could smell the coffee. "Do you have coffee?"

"Not for you," the first guard said, finally pointing the barrel toward the ground. He kept his finger on the trigger and that bothered Wolfe. They were one heartbeat from the man squeezing a .223 round in their direction. An accident would kill him just as dead. Wolfe watched the man closely.

"Just a thought. Been a long time. Maybe there is something I can trade you for?"

"You have nothing I want, but since you're coming out of the Hot Zone, you'll need to leave your contaminated contraband here."

"If you have one of those detectors, you'll see that nothing we have is radioactive."

"They said we didn't need one of those contraptions down here. They been using 'em like crazy up north, though."

"Does that mean you aren't worried about radiation down this way?"

"Are you stupid, mister? We worry about radiation all the time. You ever see what it does to people?"

"Then why don't you have a Geiger counter?"

"Because no one ever comes through this checkpoint. How dense are you?" the first soldier asked.

Wolfe positioned himself in front of Jennifer and Buddy as the dog had started to growl again. He finally put his hands down.

"Too many blows to the head. Look at those goggles!"

"Can we pass?" Wolfe looked at the soldier still holding his rifle.

"We're going to have to confiscate that rifle."

Wolfe sized up the two soldiers, just in case he needed to act. The one with the rifle pointed at his feet would be the most dangerous. He would have to kill him first, if it came to that. The other one would never be able to unsling his M16 before Wolfe could get to him.

He did not want to leave his rifle, but with the bow and a full load of arrows, he would be able to keep them fed.

"I would prefer not to leave it behind. What is it going to take to continue on my way with what little we have?"

"Can't let you go on with a hot rifle."

"I guess. I don't want trouble. We are on our way to Florida, that's it. Our home is back there. We got caught on this side during the war and are finally able to make a go of getting home. I need this rifle. I promise not to fire it in FEDCOM territory. I'll save that for the Hot Zones."

The second guard motioned for Wolfe to hand it over.

Wolfe slipped the pack off his back and removed the rifle. He looked at it for a moment, then shrugged. He punched the button and caught the magazine as it fell. He pulled the charging handle to the rear and caught the ejected .223 round. He plugged that into the magazine. He handed both the rifle and the magazine to the second solder.

"You gents have a fine evening." Wolfe waved for the

young girl to walk around the men. She took one step before the first soldier's rifle came up.

"And her."

Wolfe clenched his jaw. He had not wanted to get into a fight, but the fights always seemed to find him. He held his hands up and nodded. He crouched to talk with the youngster.

"It's going to be alright Miss Jennifer," he said softly. "These nice men will take care of you."

She started to shake, thinking Wolfe had betrayed her. He took hold of her shoulders and shook her, manhandling her to place her in front of the two men. They looked at her as men shouldn't look at children. Wolfe used the distraction to take a sidestep, too quick for the eyes to follow and ripped the rifle from the first soldier's hand. He turned the rifle into a club and hit the man so hard the stock of the weapon cracked when it smashed across the man's face.

Wolfe kept moving. The other soldier was trying to bring up the AR-15, but dropped the magazine while trying to stuff it into the rifle. He bent down and Wolfe kicked him so hard that it nearly took the man's head off. The snapping of his neckbones told the story of his death.

Wolfe returned to the first soldier to pick him up by his head and finish him with a twist and jerk.

"We have about two hours to be a long ways away from here."

Jennifer stared dumbly at the carnage that Wolfe had wrought in the space of only a few heartbeats.

"I'll be needing this more than you," Wolfe told the dead man before he picked up his AR-15, slapped the magazine home, and chambered a round. He pulled the FEDCOM issued M16 off the man's shoulder and handed it to Jennifer.

"I'm sorry, Mister Wolfe," she apologized, tears glistening in her eyes. "I thought you were going to leave me."

"Miss Jennifer," he shook his head. "I keep my promises. I told you that you were family. I wouldn't hand Buddy over to the scum at Canon City, and I sure as hell won't be handing you over to the scum of FEDCOM."

She took the rifle, unsure what to do with it.

"Protect yourself. I'll teach you how to handle it once we're out there." He pointed south, into the rolling flatlands, not east along the road.

"Maybe they'll think these two got in a fight and killed each other?" she offered.

"Then we'll have to put the rifle back."

She did not hesitate to lay it across the man.

"But not here. If they got into a fight, it would be by the fire." Wolfe looked the area over. He went into the shack and shut off the floodlight, happy to be able to remove his goggles. He went to the fire and poured himself a cup of coffee. He took a sip. It wasn't much better than motor oil, complete with grounds, but it was the best coffee he had had in ages.

Jennifer tried to drag one of the soldiers, but Wolfe called to her to stop.

"Get the rifle and gear. I will move the men."

They arranged them near the fire. Wolfe took the one man's boot and stomped it hard across the other's throat. He picked up a rock and crushed the skull of the man with the damaged face.

He arranged the evidence as best he could and waved to Jennifer. There were two ration packs on a bench near the fire.

She reached for them but he stopped her.

"Leave them. If we take anything that they are supposed to have, FEDCOM will know. For once, they never saw us. They can't be on the lookout for someone they don't know exists."

Jennifer took one last look at the ration packs. She scratched buddy behind his ears. When she looked back up, her eyes were clear and her face set.

"Lead the way, Mister Wolfe."

ABOUT THE AUTHOR

Frank Roderus wrote his first story—it was a western—when he was five. It was really awful, as might be expected, but his mother kept that typed and spell-checked short story tucked away until the day she died.

Later, Frank became a newspaper reporter, thinking that books are written by authors which he most assuredly was not. He kept trying to write though, and eventually did it wrong enough to learn how to get it right. That first sale, a young adult novel published by Independence Press, was more than thirty years and a good many books ago.

As a journalist, the Colorado Press Association awarded Frank Roderus their highest award, the Sweepstakes Award, for the best news story of 1980, and the Western Writers of America has twice named Frank recipient of their prestigious Spur Award.

Frank passed away at age 73 in December 2015.

NOTES - CRAIG MARTELLE
WRITTEN APRIL 19, 2019

Thank you for reading this far! You have my sincere appreciation for sticking with us and reading our stories.

The fourth Nightwalker has come to a close! I hope you didn't notice where Frank left off and I picked up the story. If you did, I hope that you were okay with it. I write in a different style, but am trying to flex to better follow Frank.

I have four more stories in mind should we want to follow Jim Wolfe on his trek home. I have a rough outline done on Nightwalker 5. He'll be going through a massive Clear Area and that's where he'll find out what's really going on. At least in that one enclave.

Frank Roderus passed away in 2015 but he lives in every word he wrote. You get a glimpse of the man in each of these stories as Frank put himself there, in a world torn apart by war, divided by those who have power, suffered by those without. I hope that I've done Frank justice with my touch ups on these stories. If you can't tell the difference, then I have done my job in helping make these post-apoc tales good for the 21st Century.

Winter has returned, but it's Alaska and it's April. Of

course, it's going to snow again. Come May, maybe we won't get any more snow. My rhubarb doesn't care. It seems to grow quite well with snow on its leaves. I planted two new bunches last summer and despite one dying early, both have popped out and are reaching for the eventual sunshine. All three of my plants are alive and kicking. We'll see what perennials show up out of the garden. I expect the mint will be there as usual, but we planted a couple other herbs that may or may not show.

We shall see.

Phyllis the Arctic Dog is doing great. She likes this time of year when temps fluctuate between 30F and 50F, but then there's the mud. She avoids much of it, but still needs a complete wipe down before going back in the house. We had a ruffed grouse show up in the yard. These are fairly rare where we live, but Phyllis didn't care. She still chased it and made it fly. It didn't go very far. For a pitbull, Phyllis isn't too scary.

That's all I have for now. Thank you again for coming on this journey with us.

Have a great day.

BOOKS BY CRAIG MARTELLE

Craig Martelle's other books (listed by series)

<u>Terry Henry Walton Chronicles</u> (co-written with Michael Anderle) – a post-apocalyptic paranormal adventure

<u>Gateway to the Universe</u> (co-written with Justin Sloan & Michael Anderle) – this book transitions the characters from the Terry Henry Walton Chronicles to The Bad Company

<u>The Bad Company</u> (co-written with Michael Anderle) – a military science fiction space opera

<u>End Times Alaska</u> (also available in audio) – a Permuted Press publication – a post-apocalyptic survivalist adventure

<u>The Free Trader</u> – a Young Adult Science Fiction Action Adventure

<u>Cygnus Space Opera</u> – A Young Adult Space Opera (set in the Free Trader universe)

<u>Darklanding</u> (co-written with Scott Moon) – a Space Western

<u>Rick Banik</u> – Spy & Terrorism Action Adventure

<u>Become a Successful Indie Author</u> – a non-fiction work

Enemy of my Enemy (co-written with Tim Marquitz) – a galactic alien military space opera

Superdreadnought (co-written with Tim Marquitz) – a military space opera

Metal Legion (co-written with Caleb Wachter) - a military space opera

End Days (co-written with E.E. Isherwood) – a post-apocalyptic adventure

Mystically Engineered (co-written with Valerie Emerson) – dragons in space

Monster Case Files (co-written with Kathryn Hearst) – a young-adult cozy mystery series

For a complete list of books from Craig, please see www.craigmartelle.com